BY LOVE RESTORED

Nancy Olander Johanson

**is an imprint of
Guideposts Associates, Inc.
Carmel, NY 10512**

By Love Restored
Copyright © 1985 by Nancy O. Johanson

This Guideposts edition is published by special arrangement with
Zondervan Publishing House.

ISBN 0-310-46862-0

Edited by Pamela M. Jewell
Designed by Kim Koning

Printed in the United States of America

For Jennifer, architect extraordinaire, with pride and love, and thanks for inspiration

CHAPTER 1

BUMPED FOR THE UMPTEENTH TIME on the crowded sidewalk, Brittany Lawson edged her way cautiously through the maze of rushing pedestrians and headed for the safety offered by the shop windows that formed the exterior of Macy's Department Store on Stockton Street. San Francisco was always alive with enthusiastic natives and tourists, but on this particular April day, it seemed unusually so.

Pausing beside a young couple peering through a store window, Brittany turned to regard the jostling throng. Everyone seemed to be in a bubbling state of expectancy, hurrying here and there with carefree abandon. The weather had something to do with it, of course. The City—as its inhabitants fondly called it—was impossible to resist once the summer fog had burned off, leaving a crisp view of the famous hills and picturesque waterfront.

But, it wasn't the weather or the city exciting the masses today. Not if she was interpreting people's faces correctly. Faces of every age were filled with the glory of spring, and new beginnings, and the euphoria of love.

Almost unaware, Brittany searched for a familiar face she hadn't seen for almost five years. There was no good reason for her to imagine she would find it among the throng walking the streets of San Francisco, but anything was possible, and on days like this, the yearning to feast on it for even a second was overpowering.

Two by two the endless stream of couples maneuvered past her. Feeling depressingly alone, she turned her back to them and gazed through the window at Macy's newest display. A waxen bride modeled an exquisite wedding gown of ivory satin and lace, encrusted with a lavish seeding of tiny pearls. Her frozen face was partially hidden under the fullness of a filmy veil that fell with teasing beguilement from a small crown placed with regal precision atop her carefully coiffed blond hair. She was beautiful . . . a perfect example of how every prospective bride hoped to look on her wedding day.

Brittany sighed wistfully, and shifted her attention to the reflection in the window of the couple by her side. Once, she had viewed bridal displays with an eagerness not unlike the young lady clutching the arm of her companion. It had been April then, too, and she had looked with equally soulful anticipation toward becoming a June bride.

Shutting out the ardent comments of the happy couple, Brittany moved lethargically down the street, sternly reminding herself there was no place for a man in her life anymore. She couldn't afford to become sentimental over the sight of a wedding dress. She could have spring fever, but she mustn't let her imagination or her emotions get out of control. She was alone by choice, and she had cut herself off from the easy access of a supportive family and past friends out of necessity. Distance from the East Coast was of paramount importance to her peace of mind, and anyway, it was clearly to her advantage to be free of

8

additional encumbrances in her personal life. Her career goals needed devoted attention, and most of the time her challenging work and achievements provided all the excitement and fulfillment she needed to be content.

Impulsively, Brittany entered Macy's and walked briskly toward the department that carried her favorite designer clothes. She didn't often indulge herself, but today she needed a morale booster. And there was no denying a new outfit could brighten her outlook and uplift her spirits.

Thirty minutes later, she glanced at her watch and laughed silently. It hadn't taken long to lighten not only her spirits, but the balance in her checkbook. Completely carried away she had purchased not one, but three new outfits, including a gorgeous, very feminine, Nipon party dress.

Clutching the shopping bag with her purchases, Brittany pushed her way through the store and out onto the sun-drenched street. Even if she ran the entire way, she would be late getting back to the office; but, since her shopping expedition was contrary to her usual pattern of fastidious punctuality, she felt certain she would be forgiven. She maneuvered her way carefully through the steady stream of shoppers, and this time, met happy faces with one of her own. The fleeting vision of a face she had once loved was again filed away in the back of her mind.

Flushed from the vigor of her rapid walk, Brit stopped immediately inside the door of the suite of rooms she shared with her associates and staff, and leaned against the wall in a dramatic show of fatigue. She heaved an exaggerated sigh and grinned at the curious stares of the receptionist and one of the office secretaries.

When one of them looked pointedly at the wall clock, Brit held up her shopping bag. "Don't say a word, Donna Greene. It wasn't my fault. Place the entire blame on spring fever. It's terribly belated, to be sure, but it got a strange hold on me today and wouldn't let go until I had bought three magnificent new outfits. Wait until you see them!"

Her friends laughed with her, as they always did. When Brittany laughed, the dimples in her cheeks deepened, and her dark brown eyes glistened.

A door adjoining the reception room opened abruptly, and a portly gentleman, with Franklin glasses balanced on the edge of his Romanesque nose, peered over the frames at them. "Brittany, I'm glad you're back. Could you come into my office when you're ready, please?"

Brit sobered immediately. "Of course, sir. I'm sorry to be so late." Rushing forward to hand her packages to Donna, she added, "Find someone to take these down to my car, will you? I left the keys with the garage attendant." She strode into the next room shutting the door behind her. "I hope I haven't kept you waiting, Lewis."

"No one's watching the clock, Brittany. Your lunch time is your own. Whatever you did to bring back that beautiful smile, however, I heartily approve of it. You haven't been yourself these past few days. I've missed your cheerfulness." Lewis smiled at her indulgently.

"Thanks. It was only a touch of belated spring fever, I think. It should be nicely cured, if the price of those new outfits I bought means anything." Brit laughed again, and dropped gracefully onto the end of a small couch to one side of the massive mahogany desk that quite effectively minimized the girth of her employer.

Lewis Stanford III, headed a world-renowned firm of architects, Lewis Stanford and Associates, based in San Francisco. He was an exceptionally gifted architect, known for his commitment to progress, his ingenious use of open space, and his sometimes sharp break with the conventions of the times while attempting to reuse history and make it something uniquely American. Since he had already made his mark as a master builder, and enjoyed both artistic and commerical achievement, he had turned his interest, and considerable influence, toward the preservation of historic properties. Through his efforts, there were an increasing number of historic districts being established throughout California, especially in San Francisco, and these were safeguarded by historic zoning designations.

It was his reputation for restoring, or renovating, the old Victorian homes in San Francisco, in particular, that had brought Brittany to the city to seek a position in his firm almost five years ago. She had the right qualifications, and Lewis had been impressed and even a little excited about the projects in her portfolio.

Within a matter of weeks, their friendship and mutual admiration had blossomed into a warm kinship, taking on the semblance of a father-daughter relationship. Brittany adored the venerable, natural-born executive, and trusted his judgment implicitly. He had great dignity, and rarely raised his low, cultivated voice above a normal conversational level. Only a few minutes in his presence, a few well-chosen words from his lips, and most people were listening intently. He was inspirational and instructive, highly intelligent, and interested in everything going on about him.

Lewis removed the dark-rimmed glasses from his nose and placed them on the pile of papers cluttering the desk top. He rubbed the reddened spot where they had rested before his eyes finally focused on Brittany.

"I've lined up an exciting project for you, my dear. It's tailor-made for your expertise, and, if my hunch is right, its successful completion should bring you the well-earned recognition of both your peers and the general public."

When he finished speaking, he rocked in his oversized leather chair, hooked an arm over a back corner, and grinned, obviously pleased with Brit's stunned expression. He knew he had established a captive audience.

Brittany leaned forward, her widened eyes never leaving his face. "Well? Go on. Don't you dare keep me in suspense! It's got to be a restoration project. Is it?"

Lewis laughed again and pulled open a desk drawer to extract an old briar pipe and a leather-zippered pouch of tobacco.

Brittany leapt up to snatch both items from his hands. "Oh, no you don't! I refuse to sit here while you go through that slow, tedious process of filling, tamping and lighting up. You'll get this paraphernalia back when you 'fess up.' " She sank back onto the couch and crossed her arms over her chest, one item clutched in each hand.

Lewis threw up his hands in surrender. "All right, all right. I'll make it quick." He rocked for a few seconds, drumming his fingers on the chair arm. "You know the old Henry Casebolt house on Pierce Street?"

"Of course I know it!" Brittany sat up as though shocked by an electric current. "It's been up for sale for six and a half months for an outrageous sum; I inquired about it the first day I saw the sign. I drive by it every day on my way to the office. I've been *drooling* with desire to handle the rebirth of that fantastic house. Has it sold? Do you know who bought it? Lewis, you *aren't* trying to tell me that . . ."

Lewis nodded, feeling her excitement and enjoying his role in it. "Yes, I know who bought it; and yes, he's called to ask this firm to handle the restoration. I told him we'd be delighted, that I had a young associate who specialized in such projects, and that I could guarantee it would be one of the finest restorations in the history of San Francisco. I want you to handle the project from beginning to end by yourself this time. It'll be your masterpiece or your Waterloo. It's time for you to make your name known in the books of architecture."

"This is almost too much to take in all at once." Brit placed the pipe and pouch on the desk and peered down at them as though in a trance. When she saw and felt the warm, slightly calloused hands patting her own pale ones, she raised her dark lashes and revealed the nervousness and fear that were putting a knot in her stomach. "Do you think I'm ready, Lewis?"

"As ready as any architect on my staff, Brittany dear. You're extremely gifted, and all you need to develop is an unshakable faith in your concepts and in your ability to carry them to fruition. I'm not going to abandon you. I'll be right here if you need me."

"Well, of course I'll need you. I'll always need you. I don't know how I could have made it through these past five years without your interest and help. You're responsible for leading me back to the Lord. You provided me with the secret to your personal and business success. Remember? *'Trust in the Lord with all thine heart; and lean not unto thine own understanding. In all thy ways acknowledge him, and he shall direct thy paths.'* "

Brit swallowed a lump in her throat and turned to walk toward the windows lining one wall. She peered blindly through the beige, gauze draperies. "I believe God brought me to this moment through your loving guidance, Lewis, so why do I feel . . . sort of . . . lost and alone? I feel like I'm being kicked out of the fold into the hard cruel world, and I never felt this way when I left my parents to go off to college. It's totally ridiculous, you know. I'm a mature, full-fledged woman of twenty-six." She choked on her words and fiddled with a button on her grass-green, Chanel-styled suit jacket.

"Come here, Brittany. Come and sit down. If you keep standing, then I'll have to get up, and my feet are bothering me today." Lewis motioned for her to return to the couch. "That's better. I want to apologize for throwing in that unnecessary Waterloo idea. I don't believe for even one fraction of a second you have a chance at failure on this project, dear. I've been in this business for more years than I care to admit, and I don't exaggerate when I say you're destined to go down in history. Your eye for what needs to be done in the restoration of our wonderful old structures of architectural integrity is unsurpassed, in my opinion. Don't be afraid to take risks and be assertive when you know you're right."

Brittany had lowered her eyes to study the pattern on her shirt during the latter part of Lewis's praise, but raised them now to return his smile of encouragement. "Thank you, Lewis. I hope I can live up to such effusive kudos. I'll give it my best try, for your sake, as well as mine." She sighed deeply, paused for only a fraction of a second, and then grinned impishly. "Now, tell me everything!"

A grey cloud of pipe smoke hovered in the space between them, and Lewis Stanford waved it aside with one hand. "I don't know much more myself. We're to meet the owner at the house in less than an hour. I'll go over there with you to make introductions, and then leave the details for the two of you to work out. You know our business policies and fees. The rest is up to you. I'll have the car brought around to the front of the office in twenty minutes. Can you be ready?"

"I'm ready now. If I spend too much time thinking about it, I'll get cold feet." On an impulse, she walked around the desk and planted a kiss on his brow. "Thank you for everything, Lewis, not only for this dream of an opportunity. I can't begin to express my gratitude." She smiled at him with misty eyes.

"It has been my pleasure, dear, and Marion feels the same way. She loves you like the daughter she never had. I spoke with her after lunch today and mentioned the Casebolt House. She's as ecstatic as you, and asked me to extend an invitation for dinner tonight to celebrate. Can you make it at seven o'clock, or have you made other plans?"

"Even if I had, I'd cancel them for one of Miss Marion's marvelous dinners. Tell her I'd be delighted to come."

"Good, I'll call her now." He turned to telephone his wife, and Brittany slipped out of his office and into her own.

There, in quiet solitude, she bowed her head and allowed a few tears to roll down her smooth cheeks.

Lord, I stand before You at this moment, an exceedingly happy and thankful woman, but I'm sure you can hear the knocking of my knees! I'm scared stiff! You and I formed a living partnership five years ago, and not once have You reneged on Your part of our agreement. When I came to You, heartsore, and in need of a friend, You opened your arms with no questions asked. You gave me the comfort and guidance of the Holy Spirit, and led me to the promises in Your Word: 'Delight thyself also in the Lord; and He shall give thee the desires of thine heart. Commit thy way unto the Lord; trust also in Him; and He shall bring it to pass.'

I've wanted so much! And Lord, I certainly haven't been Your most faithful partner. Many times I've been so caught up in my own importance, I've taken all the credit when things blossomed, and blamed You for abandoning me when things went wrong. Right now, I want to give You the credit You deserve—all of it. You gave me talent, and then You continuously opened doors to provide the means to develop it; You tirelessly came to my aid when I was ready to give up, and gave me new strength, and the desire to set high goals. I can't thank You enough for all that.

You've also known for a long time how much I love the Henry Casebolt house, Lord, and probably why, although I don't. Some mysterious feeling, deep within me, made my interest in it grow, and I've harbored this secret urge to restore it into a new home. Now, I've been handed the responsibility, and I'm overwhelmed by my inadequacies! Thank You for the gift of this golden opportunity, though. I'm not at all worthy of Your unceasing generosity, Lord, and it's only because I know firsthand of Your limitless love that I selfishly ask for your continued blessing now. I'm petrified that I'll make mistakes and ruin that wonderful house! I need You as my partner, and I humbly remember the warning from the Scriptures . . . 'Except the Lord build the house, they labor in vain that build it.'

Brittany and Lewis walked up the steps of the historic Casebolt House and rang the bell for entry. Brit heaved a sigh and tried to consciously stem the churning in her stomach.

"Nice place," said Lewis in a quiet aside. "I've always liked the looks of it. I think Henry Casebolt built it in 1865. It's considered the finest example in the city of that period of incredible growth."

Brittany had her back turned to the door when it opened, perusing the neighboring houses. She heard male voices and turned at the same time Lewis tugged on her sleeve.

"You'll have to forgive my associate's distraction, young man. This house holds a special place in her heart, and she's a little overcome by the prospect of returning it to its former beauty. Allow me to introduce the two of you." Lewis drew Brittany into the expansive entrance hall. "Brittany Lawson, meet your new business partner for the next few months, Mr. Mitchell Newmann.''

Brittany was struck dumb. She could feel alternate waves of hot and cold suffuse her body, and hear a roaring in her ears. It couldn't be true. *He* couldn't be the new owner of *her* house! For five long years she had wondered how she would handle the situation if ever they should meet again, and now she knew. The pain was still there, as profuse and suffocating as it had been when she first found out his secret. And if she weren't careful, she would succumb to it and give herself away.

The floor seemed to give way under her feet, and for a paralyzing moment she thought she would drop out of sight before she could acknowledge his presence. She almost welcomed the thought, before tucking a hasty arm around one of Lewis Stanford's, gripping the sleeve of his jacket in an attempt to steady her shattered nerves.

Another shock jolted her when she raised her leaden lashes to meet Mitchell Newmann's gaze. ''So, we meet again, Miss Lawson.'' His eyes were as gray as a San Francisco fog and they successfully concealed his feelings from her. He was aware of her discomfort, and the smile that stretched the taut, bronzed skin of his cheeks seemed to mock her inability to speak. His dark, heavy brows lifted in silent amusement, and she was loath to admit he still had the power to rule her emotions.

Brittany ran a quick tongue over her dry lips and compelled herself to respond with more warmth than she felt. She was no longer a socially inept school girl. She would show him from the very outset that she was in control of this awkward situation.

''For heaven's sake, Mr. Newmann, I can't believe it's you! How long has it been—four, five years? What are you doing out here on the West Coast?'' She offered her hand in an overly vigorous shake, pulling

17

it free of his scalding one to tuck into the pocket of her jacket before its trembling became visible to him.

Lewis Stanford exchanged glances with both of them. "Do you two know each other? What a needless question. I don't suppose you'd care to fill me in?"

Forcing a gay little bubble of laughter, Brittany moved closer to him for moral support and offered an explanation. "It was in Baltimore, wasn't it, Mr. Newmann? I worked on a project of yours out there, when I was still a student. It was called Harborplace, or something like that."

She was being deliberately vague and he responded in kind. "Something like that."

Lewis beamed. "Then I don't need to waste time extolling the excellence of Brittany's talent, Mr. Newmann. I'm sure you need no reminders."

"Yes, Miss Lawson has quite unforgettable talent. Is she the associate you mentioned in our phone conversation?"

Brit felt derision in his voice, and knew it was lost on Lewis, who had no reason to suspect the enmity between them.

"Yes, she is. There's no finer restoration architect in this entire city for what you have in mind here, Mr. Newmann. I will stake my reputation on her work any day."

"I don't think he can be expected to have any confidence in me, Lewis. After all, I don't have very many years experience for such an enormous and costly project. Why don't you assign one of your other architects. . .Mr. Kennedy, for instance." The sharpness of Brittany's interruption brought a scowl to the face of her mentor.

"Nonsense, dear. You're perfect for this job."

"I agree with you, sir. I'm quite satisfied to have Miss Lawson handle the restoration of Casebolt House. There's no need to consider anyone else."

Brittany felt a rush of irrational anger. Mitch had no right to pressure her into something she didn't want to do! "Now that I see the house, I really don't think I'm ready to handle such a difficult project on my own, Lewis."

"Of course you're ready. It's all settled. I'll leave the two of you to tour the place and define the extent of the renovation. You don't need me to put in my two cents worth." Chuckling with pleasure over his attempt at humor, Lewis offered his hand. "Mr. Newmann, it's been a pleasure to meet you. I'm a great admirer of your ventures to revitalize the wastelands of our country's major cities. They're innovative and praiseworthy. The transformations you've already masterminded, in re-energizing various downtown areas, show an uncanny ability. I'm all for it, son. Keep it up. We need to reshape our thinking about city life."

"Thank you, sir. From what I've read about you, I'd say we have the same philosophy—a desire to meet the needs of the people."

Lewis smoothed his tie over the paunch of his rather rotund abdomen, and nodded agreeably. "Gives a man a good feeling, too. We're helping to restore a profound sense of community spirit in the inner city. So is Brittany, bless her heart. She's making a worthy contribution herself. She might not be a nationally recognized expert of urban problems like you, but her enthusiasm and talent for restoring San Francisco's Victorian homes is going to establish her name very soon. Well, I've kept you from getting on with your work long enough. I'll get back to the office and let you begin."

"*Wait*, Lewis!" Brittany called after him with a note of near panic in her voice. "I-I need to go back with you. I don't have my own car here, *remember?*"

"That's all right, Miss Lawson. I'll drive you back downtown when we have finished our business."

Mitchell Newmann's offer successfully overrode her feeble attempt to escape being left alone with him, and Lewis waved a cheerful farewell and motioned his chauffeur to drive off.

The silence that ensued was almost deafening. Brittany raised one tremulous hand to still the pounding in her temples. Conscious of Mitchell's close proximity, she sucked in a ragged breath of air and turned to face him with as much false courage as she could muster under the circumstances.

"Shall we get on with the tour, Mr. Newmann? No doubt you're a busy man." She met his gaze boldly, but was inwardly shocked by the granite hardness and godlike virility of his well-remembered features. A museum sculpture contained more compassion than he was exhibiting. But even at thirty-eight, every inch of his tall frame was still as muscular as before, and exuded more strength and breath-snatching eye appeal than any man's physical appearance had a right to do.

"In a minute, Miss Lawson. We have a few things to discuss first." Mitch peered down at her with cool insolence. "The proper restoration of Casebolt House means a great deal to me. For the first time in several years, I plan to be with my family full time. Since the project I've undertaken in San Francisco is an ambitious one, involving a minimum of three to five years to complete, I don't want to spend every weekend flying to Denver to be with them."

He paused briefly, eyeing her without changing the lines of his face. "I agree with Lewis Stanford. You do have exceptional talent in restoration work, and I know from personal observation you can be fast and efficient. I need someone with those particular qualities right now. But, your shortcomings concern me." He paused again, and his face hardened. "You run out on commitments, Miss Lawson. You leave people high and dry, without explanations. I won't tolerate such behavior on this project! Once you begin work on this house, you'll stay to finish it, or there'll be a consequence to pay. Is that clear?''

Brittany's eyes wavered under the intensity of Mitchell's unspoken threat. But she stood her ground and answered in her uniquely husky voice. ''Perfectly, sir; but, I'd like an opportunity to set the record straight first. I have never run out on a commitment, because when I make a promise to someone, I keep it! I've only left one 'situation' without an explanation. It wasn't necessary, under the circumstances.'' Her voice rose. ''If there is anything I absolutely abhor, it's a liar and cheat!''

''What's that supposed to mean!''

''It shouldn't be difficult to figure out! It's self-explanatory.'' Brittany moved and began an aggressive examination of the room, knowing Mitch's eyes were following her with close scrutiny. How could she bear to work for him again, when every second in his presence shattered her nerves? It was torture to even think of restoring this dream house for him to share with someone else.

On the other hand, seeing him often was better than daydreaming about where he was and wondering what he was doing. Had he missed her at all? Had he tried to find her?

Fighting the impulse unsuccessfully, Brit turned her head to steal another look at him. Both his hands were slipped into the pockets of grey dress slacks. *He's still so heart-stoppingly gorgeous!* She could feel the heat of a rapid flush that began with her neck and rose to cover her face. Her eyes met Mitch's intense gaze and they stared at each other for a long searching moment, mute, except for the messages transmitted by their eyes.

Through a daze of emotional upheaval, she heard his harsh whisper. ''Why did you leave me, Brit?''

His voice parted the ghost riders of her painful

memories. She didn't want to relive them. What was the use? Angry with him for making their reunion more punishing by daring to bring up the past, she ignored his question and curtly asked a more impersonal one of her own. "Would you like a faithful restoration of each room, Mr. Newmann, or a complete gutting with modern adaptations? Personally, I feel it would be a shame to do that. This house is almost a textbook of the style."

"You know more about old houses than I do, Miss Lawson," Mitch said at length, his voice steady again. "Do what you please; I only ask that you get it done well, and as quickly as possible. Hire yourself some decorators you can work with when the structural work is taken care of. I want the place furnished properly down to the last detail. I'll open an account in your name at the bank that Stanford's firm uses. Take charge of everything. I'll see that you are properly paid for your services."

"Fine. When do you plan to move your . . . f-family . . . here?" Had he heard her choke? Would he understand how much it hurt her to talk about it?

"As soon as you have a few rooms at least marginally livable," he replied tersely, striding into the next room.

Brit followed him, admiring his regal carriage, the width of his shoulders, the narrowness of his hips, and, as always, the long, lean length of his legs. He hated her and she loved him, still. She would always love him. There wasn't another man on earth who could come even close to filling her heart with love as he had.

"Then I'll begin indoors with the kitchen and a few bedrooms. I understand Henry Casebolt built this house for his wife and eleven children. H-how many bedrooms should I prepare, and are there any in particular you'd . . . ?" Her voice faded, and she cleared her throat.

22

"Three. You choose. Let's go. I'll drive you back to the office now. You don't need me to show you around. I'll give you a set of keys and you can come and go as you please."

Three. Does he have a son now? Or another daughter? Responding to his remark, Brittany answered, "But, this is your house. You should decide how you want it restored."

"You're the restoration expert."

"But, your wife . . ."

Mitch stopped and pivoted so abruptly that they collided. His hands shot out to steady her, gripping her arms like bands of steel. "What about my wife?" he rasped.

"W-won't she have a preference?"

"No!"

Brittany found it difficult to breath. Mitch's nearness made her legs weak, and her arms were tingling from his touch. She felt the traitorous undercurrents of old dormant feelings, and knew she should do something to free herself from his grasp. "I'll do my best, then, and . . ." Her mouth was dry and it was difficult to speak.

Mitch's strong pulse was visible through the tanned skin of his neck. It distracted her, and she swallowed convulsively.

Suddenly, she was hauled into Mitch's arms, and with a strangled, *"Brit!"* he was kissing her with a fierceness that made her powerless to do anything but respond in kind. Nothing had changed. She met his passion with incoherent gasps of pure joy, entangling her fingers into the thickness of his crisp, dark hair, and revelling in its recalled sensuousness. It was indescribably wonderful being in his arms again.

Mitch's lips burned a trail down the side of one cheek and across an almost hidden ear, lingering to whisper loving words.

"Brit, Brit." His mouthing of her name sounded

tortured. "You've bewitched me again, darling. You're so incredibly beautiful. So much more than I remembered." He held her tightly, as though fearing she would disappear if he loosened his grip on her. "I can't begin to tell you how much I've missed you, my dark-eyed gypsy. I've dreamed of this moment a thousand times. I-I can't believe . . ." His voice thickened, and giving up on words, he possessed her lips again.

What was she doing? How could she forget the reason for their separation? Their passion for each other hadn't changed with the passage of time, but Mitch was married, wasn't he? He was bringing his family to this very house! "No! *Stop* it, Mitch!" She pushed at him with ineffectual hands, pulling her lips away from his.

"What do you mean, 'no?'" Mitch lifted his head slowly, and a puzzled look replaced the glazed one, revealing the depths of his emotional involvement.

"W-what kind of man are you, Mitch? You have a daughter!" she sputtered indignantly. "Y-you're a—a family man!"

"Are you saying that matters to you? It never crossed my mind you were the sort of woman to hold an innocent child against a man!"

"Well, you're mistaken. Of course it matters!"

"I don't recall your behaving like it mattered."

"You didn't tell me! You kept it secret!" Aghast at the volume and force of her responses, Brit took a long, heaving breath, counted to ten, and mentally ordered herself to calm down. "You conveniently omitted several choice tidbits of important information from your conversations with me," she continued, her eyes glued to his. "I had to find out by myself, and it was fortunate for me that I did, before it was too late. I-I saw the pictures in your hotel apartment."

"And so you left without asking for a single word of

explanation." Mitch raked his fingers through his nutmeg-colored hair, staring at her, and accusing and condemning her with his polished, steel eyes.

"I didn't need any of your explanations, Mitchell Newmann. The inscriptions on the photographs said it all. 'Yours forever, your loving wife,' 'I love you, Daddy.'" Brittany's voice mimicked a child's, and the bitterness of five years curled her lip.

Mitch's eyes narrowed. "What could you possibly have against an innocent little girl?"

"You're despicable! I wasn't interested in some relationship with a family man! You should have told me before I allowed myself to fall so . . . so hopelessly . . . Oh, never mind." She pushed the tumbled mass of black curls from her face, and tucked her rumpled blouse more securely into her skirt with jerking motions.

"All right, now that I have my belated explanation of your sudden disappearance from my life, I won't bother you again," Mitch said coldly. "Get this house ready for occupancy as quickly as possible, Miss Lawson, and we can conclude our association with each other permanently."

"That day can't come soon enough for me." Brittany brushed angry tears from her eyes and walked briskly across the empty room, each click of her heels clattering loudly. She turned at the door. "If it won't be too difficult for you to spend a few more minutes in my presence, I'd like that ride back to my office now, Mr. Newmann."

Several minutes later, Brittany stood on the sidewalk in front of Lewis Stanford and Associates clutching a ring of keys, shivering in the warm April sunshine, and wondering why she felt so completely bereft. It was as though a belated blast of winter's icy breath had suddenly stripped her nude, freezing her soul in its wake.

She felt empty, lifeless, dead. Why, *why* had fate

sent Mitchell Newmann to San Francisco and into her very own dream house?

Dear Father in Heaven, five years ago I thought I had met an enemy on the battlefield of life, and I successfully used my inner strength to fight it. I sought Your forgiveness. I learned to deal with my guilt and to forgive myself. Why has it returned to haunt me now? Forgive me again for my weakness where Mitch is concerned. I still can't control my subconscious mind, or rationalize the depth of feeling I have for him. You'll have to do it for me.

CHAPTER 2

BRITTANY TRIED TO RISE ABOVE her unwelcome, but persistent depression as she dressed for dinner. Several times, she picked up the telephone receiver to dial Marion Stanford and beg off for the evening, but she came to her senses in time to keep herself from making the feeble excuses that were certain to make the elderly woman suspicious. It was ridiculous enough that she hadn't returned to her office after being dropped off by Mitch, but she felt incapable of facing anyone, especially Lewis. He was bound to ask about her afternoon sooner or later, however, so it made no sense to make a bad situation worse by cancelling the thoughtful, and well-intentioned dinner invitation.

Why did things happen the way they did? She had tried to burn her bridges behind her and begin a new life free of any compunctions regarding Mitchell Newmann, but it had proven an impossibility. He wasn't the kind of man she could easily forget. He was her Achilles heel. How could she get through the next few weeks knowing she might see him again at any moment of the day to discuss making her dream project—the Casebolt house—a home for him and his family? Even thinking about it filled her with helpless anger and frustration. Life wasn't at all fair.

Feeling ready to blow up, Brittany pulled off her shoes and threw them across the bedroom of her small second-floor apartment, hearing the thud against the thin wallboard with only a trace of satisfaction. There would have been a great deal more satisfaction if the shoes had connected with Mitch Newmann's body! He was a conceited, lying two-timer who treated women like objects of no more value than—than marshmallows! He was despicable. His wife was welcome to him.

Removing her suit jacket, blouse, and skirt with unnecessary roughness, and flinging them in anger to the floor, she paused to stomp on them in her stocking feet before heading to the bathroom for a shower and shampoo. If she had to go out for the evening, she would go completely cleansed of every vestige of that man's look, and touch, and scent.

Later, wrapped in a terry knee-length robe of deep pink, she pulled open the closet door and flicked hastily through her wardrobe. Nothing appealed to her. In her foul mood, she didn't think even the Crown Jewels would look good.

Brittany felt childish. Grown women—mature Christian women—didn't allow life's little disappointments to rule their actions to the point where they couldn't function at all. Every end brought a new beginning. God never closed doors without opening new ones. It was time for her to take control of circumstances, and not be a helpless victim of them! She was an architect, and understood more than others that sticks and stones, bricks and mortar were only that, until a builder made something of them. She would make a new life without Mitchell Newmann, without memories of him, in fact.

Removing her purchases from the large shopping bag she had asked Donna Greene to place in her car, Brittany threw them on her bed and reached for the dress rich in jewel tones of lapis, amethyst, topaz, and onyx. It wasn't to be compared with the Crown Jewels, but it was a treasure of a dress for the evening, made of pure silk crêpe de Chine. It might be rather luxurious for a quiet dinner with the Stanfords, but it was definitely an ego booster and morale builder. The high-necked lapis blouse with three covered buttons down the left shoulder was a perfect foil for her dark sultry looks, and the border-striped dirndl skirt hugged her with instant flattery. Substituting a belt to match her new leather pumps, she stuffed the fabric sash back into the empty sack. Tonight, she would opt for sheer elegance.

Standing in front of the full-length closet door mirror, Brittany assessed the final results with the cold, dispassionate eye of a scientist. She was pleased with what she saw. As she stood there, she thought of Mitch. She had always harbored the thought of having been too hasty and possibly even mistaken about him, but today's revelations had removed every unspoken hope of ever getting together with him again. She was *not* a home wrecker. She built them and restored them.

Twirling around, Brittany watched the silk fabric of her skirt swirl around her slender hips. She had already spent far too much time dwelling on the disappointment of losing Mitch when nothing could be done about it. God had forgiven her long ago for falling in love with a married man. She would forgive herself—and Mitch—and try to be receptive to the possible blessing of a new love in her life. So with the dawning of a new day, with the donning of a swishy, new dress, Brittany Lawson would become a new woman! And when she finished restoring Mr. Newmann's Victorian mansion, its unqualified magnificence would be recognized around the world. Her name would become a household word!

Brittany grinned once again at the image of herself in the mirror. What utter nonsense. Fixing up an old, historically significant house in San Francisco could possibly provide her with personal pride and satisfaction, but it was highly unlikely to make her even nationally known. Fame and popularity weren't worthy goals anyway, but her fantasy lifted her spirits.

Snatching up the evening bag that matched her shoes, Brittany rushed from her apartment and down to her car on winged feet, feeling a compelling need to retain her high level of positive thinking as long as possible. Driving through the city traffic would effectively divert her attention from further thoughts about any subject, and once she got to the Stanford's, she could steer the conversation to the weather, the food, or their numerous volunteer projects. It wasn't necessary to spend a single minute thinking or talking about Mitch Newmann.

Three-quarters of an hour later, she smiled warmly at the elderly servant who had pulled the door open to welcome her before her finger had even touched the bell. "How did you do that, Mrs. Chang? I didn't press the doorbell button yet!"

"I know you be here on time, Missy Rawson. You never rate, not once. You nice young woman. Don't keep old folks waiting." Closing the heavily carved door with meticulous care, the old Chinese housekeeper motioned Brittany to follow her to the living room. Mrs. Chang had been working for the Stanfords thirty or more years, and knew everything about everyone invited more than once to the house. She was very protective of her employers, fiercely loyal, and inclined to speak out regarding her prejudices without being asked. Brittany measured up to her strict standards, and was doted on whenever she visited.

"Missy *R*awson here now, Boss." Mrs. Chang made the announcement from the doorway into the spacious living room. "She wear spiffy new dress. Make her *r*ook *r*ike movie star."

Brittany laughed self-consciously and gave the startled Mrs. Chang a quick hug to cover her discomfort. "Thank you, Mrs. Chang. You know how to make a lady feel like a star, anyway."

"Brittany, my dear, we're so very happy you could join us this evening." A tiny, waiflike woman floated gracefully across the room with both arms outstretched in welcome. Mrs. Marion Stanford was a remarkable woman—strong-willed, confident, energetic, and capable of charming the skin off a rattlesnake. She claimed her size and appearance had never deterred her from accomplishing what she set out to do; in fact, it often worked in her favor. A halo of soft, pure white curls surrounded an animated face featuring the brightest, most inquisitive blue eyes Brittany had ever seen. "Look at you, young lady. Lewis, come see your lovely associate. Isn't she beautiful tonight?"

Marion raised her face to accept a kiss on the cheek, and keeping hold of Brittany's hands, smiled with genuine fondness at the woman she had unofficially adopted into her family. All the while, she examined Brit in minute detail with her profoundly practiced eye.

"Our Brittany is always beautiful." Lewis Stanford rose from the highbacked chair near the fireplace and came forward to extend his own welcome. "Is that one of your new dresses, my dear? If it is, we're mighty grateful to that belated bout of spring fever you suffered today."

"If you two don't stop it right now, I'm going to get a swelled head. I'll start believing you and dash off to Hollywood to begin a new career." Brittany scolded them affectionately.

"Don't you dare, child; we'd miss you terribly. Come and sit near the fire. There's just enough nip in the air tonight to warrant it, and I do love to sit and chat around the flickering warmth of a wood fire." Joyously upbeat, Marion directed her loving companion of forty-two years while ushering Brit across the room. Lewis chuckled at his wife's infectious demeanor, shaking his head in pretended intolerance.

Brittany's cheeks were dented with deep dimples, and some of her misgivings about the evening vanished. She settled onto the small chintz-covered loveseat near the fire and gazed abut the lovely room appreciatively.

"I can't possibly be patient tonight, Brittany. Lewis told me about the Casebolt House, and I'm thrilled beyond words that you're to have this wonderful opportunity so early in your career." Marion spoke with bubbling animation, punctuating her enthusiasm with the fluttering fingers of her dainty hands. "Tell me all about it, dear. Is the house as lovely inside as the exterior suggests? Is it in fairly decent condition? Do you have carte blanche, or must you work under a strict budget? What is Mr. Newmann like?"

"Relax, Marion. Brittany isn't going anywhere for a while. Wait until Douglas arrives. She'll just have to repeat herself otherwise."

"Is Doug Kennedy coming tonight, Miss Marion?"

"Yes, dear. After all, we're celebrating a special milestone in your life. We wanted to make it a memorable occasion for you, and what better way is there than to share it over a lovely dinner with friends who care about you? I wish your parents could be here as well, but, perhaps we can call them a little later. Or have you already?"

"No, I haven't. There wasn't time after I returned to my apartment. You're far too good to me, Miss Marion. I'm deeply touched by your thoughtfulness in planning all this today."

"It was my pleasure, Brittany. Lewis and I enjoy having you share your work with us."

"Mr. Kennedy here now, Boss." Mrs. Chang interrupted with her announcement, and only someone who knew her fairly well could hear the slight disapproval in her voice. She had advised Brittany repeatedly that Mr. Kennedy was not the man for her, and she disliked having them thrown together for any reason.

"Thank you, Mrs. Chang. Come right in, Douglas. Glad you could make it on such short notice." Lewis strode forward to shake hands with his associate.

"How are you, sir? Hello, Mrs. Stanford. I'd like to thank you for inviting me tonight. Your dinners are not-to-be-missed occasions in my datebook."

Brittany watched from the couch as Douglas Kennedy briskly crossed the room to shake hands with his hostess. She liked his pleasant, easy-going manners, his uncomplicated nature, his warmth. She had always gotten along well with him in joint projects at the office, and never hesitated to seek his opinions or help in private work. He was a good listener, a thoughtful cohort and a good friend. Many times they had shared an inexpensive meal together after a long day, and both of them used the other as a convenient 'guest' when invited to attend a function as part of a couple.

He grinned at her now. "Congratulations, Brit. The entire office is buzzing abut the plum you pulled out of the pie today. You got your wish, gal. You've got the luck of the Irish. I'm tickled pink for you." He traced a circle around his face with an extended finger, and joined the others in laughing at the crimson flush that fused the mass of freckles across his youthful countenance. "Literally, by now, if I know the traitorous sign of heat I feel up here!"

Brittany held out her hand to him and pulled him down beside her on the couch. "Never mind, Doug," she soothed, not even attempting to control the width of her smile. "I adore your blushes and your freckles . . . *and* your flashy carrot, red hair and bushy eyebrows . . . *and* your gorgeous green eyes . . ."

Covering his face with one hand, Douglas Kennedy parted two fingers and peeked out at his hostess. "Tell her to stop, Mrs. Stanford," he pleaded humorously. "She's breaking my heart."

Marion's eyes twinkled. "You know you're enjoying the torture, young man. You don't need me to run interference."

"You're wise beyond your years, my dear lady. I have no complaints where Brit is concerned. I only wish she adored more about me than my rather obvious Irish characteristics."

"I do, I do," Brittany continued in the same light vein, but when she met Doug's gaze, she read a different message there, and knew their relationship had entered a new phase for him.

"Sure is nice hearing young voices in this house! Now you can pump Brittany about the Casebolt House, darling. And while you're at it, have her tell us about the new owner. Ironically, he seems to be an old friend of hers."

Brittany's eyes flew to meet Doug's curious ones. She averted her gaze and feigned an amused laugh. "I'm afraid that's slightly exaggerated, Lewis. When I was a graduate student out in Baltimore, Mr. Newmann's firm was involved with the designing and building of a shopping pavilion there. I was assigned to do some work on the project."

"Holy Moly, you don't mean Harborplace, that fantastic twin glass dome masterpiece down in Inner Harbor!" Douglas Kennedy sat bolt upright in wide-eyed excitement. Turning to Marion, he elaborated. "It's an incredible structure, Mrs. Stanford—a two-story, block-long pavilion filled with shops, promenades, cafes and what have you. It transformed a trashy, decrepit site into a dazzling financial success for the city." He turned to Brittany once again.

"You don't mean to tell me the owner of the Casebolt House is *Mitchell Newmann?* Is he in San Francisco to do a project like Harborplace? I'd give my eye teeth to have a hand in designing something like that!"

Forcing another laugh, Brittany struggled to meet his enthusiasm without giving way to her personal feelings. "Yes, Mr. Newmann is responsible for Harborplace, and he did mention he was here to begin a new project, but I don't know any details."

"Does he tend to use local architects on his projects, Brit?" Lewis Stanford fussed with the lighting of his pipe and peered through the billows of thick smoke at her.

"He did in Baltimore, Lewis, but I really don't know if that's standard procedure for him."

"Since you're to work with him on his personal residence, dear, perhaps he won't object to your inquiring about his project. Wouldn't it be lovely if both you dear children could fulfill your hearts' desires, career-wise, through the sudden appearance of your wonderful Mr. Newmann?" Marion clasped her hands, and the spark of intrigue was easy to read on her almost line-free face.

Brittany could also read the hope written on Doug's face, and was gripped by a sinking feeling. "I don't think it's a good idea to put all your eggs in one basket, Miss Marion. I doubt if I'll be seeing much of Mr. Newmann, anyway. He gave me the door keys today, and told me to do whatever I wanted with the Casebolt House. Why don't you contact him, Lewis? Wouldn't it be better to make a more formal inquiry about his intentions?"

Lewis removed the stem of his pipe from his mouth. "Maybe you're right, dear. I'll look into the matter tomorrow. If Newmann's looking for local people, he couldn't find anyone who understands the area and its needs better than Doug." He replaced the pipe and drew a long draught of tobacco smoke through the stem.

"Telephone wants you, Boss." Mrs. Chang's voice rang clearly across the room, and Brittany smothered a giggle after viewing Doug's startled expression.

When the housekeeper disappeared with Lewis in her wake, Marion shook her head impatiently. "I shouldn't mind anymore. After thirty years, it's certainly too late to do anything about it, but sometimes I wish our dear Mrs. Chang would *whisper* her messages to us when we have guests."

Brittany was grateful for the change in subject. "You know you wouldn't change her, Miss Marion. Her little quirks are what make her so wonderful. You have a penchant for finding people, animals, and even objects that are unique, and Mrs. Chang fits that description to perfection."

"You know me better than I know myself, child. Douglas, doesn't Brittany look stunning tonight? I love those gorgeous colors on her." With lightning speed, she redirected the conversation, and Doug was more than willing to fall into step.

"I'm having difficulty keeping my eyes off her, Mrs. Stanford. Is that a new dress, Brit? It's a humdinger."

"Model it for him, dear."

"You're embarrassing me, Miss Marion. Douglas sees me every day at the office. He knows what I look like." Putting her glass down on a mahogany piecrust table near the couch, Brittany rose and made a self-conscious pirouette. "There. How's that?"

"If you wear similar outfits to the office, dear, I don't understand how the men can get anything accomplished. Perhaps we should do something to make a star of you. Wouldn't that be exciting? I know a producer in Hollywood, a couple directors, even the owner of a modeling agency in New York." Carried away with her new idea, Marion was unaware of Lewis' return.

"What utter nonsense, Marion. Brittany isn't a piece of fluff. She has genuine talent, and a fine reputation in architecture will live forever. It won't be threatened by some transient whim from a generally fickle public." Lewis extended a hand to his wife and pulled her to her feet, dropping a quick kiss onto her pink cheek. "We have another guest coming to share this gala evening with us, my dear. You'll need to direct Mrs. Chang in setting another place at the dinner table. That phone call was from Mitchell Newmann. I invited him to join us. He's only five minutes away at the Mark Hopkins Hotel."

"How delightful!" Marion beamed at her husband's news, and whisked out of the room, leaving only the scent of her Muguet's Lily of the Valley perfume.

Doug grinned and winked at Brittany, blind to her loss of color. "How about that! Looks like the luck of the Irish might come to me tonight, too."

"A soft drink, Doug? We'll push back dinner a few minutes and give Newmann an opportunity to relax after he arrives. I imagine he's had himself quite a busy day."

"A small glass, Lewis. Brit, anything for you?"

"No . . . wait. Yes, I'll have a glass of water." She slowly crossed the room to the fireplace, grasping hold of the mantle with one hand to steady her shaking. Her nerves were completely frazzled.

Mitch is coming to the Stanford's. Why did he call them? Does he know I'm here? Somehow, she had to hide her feelings and pray he wouldn't reveal exactly how well they knew each other . . .*had* known each other. In retrospect, she didn't know him at all.

Glancing back for just a moment and taking the glass of water, Brittany saw concern in Doug's eyes. "Are you okay, Brit?"

"You worry too much," Brit scoffed with false bravado, as she turned back to face the fire.

As her two associates engaged in a low conversation, throwing concerned looks in her direction, Brittany studied the fire, deep in thought. Much of the depression she had felt when last leaving Mitch had returned to haunt her. It was taking more energy than she could muster to squelch the desire to run away again. Maybe if she were to confide in Lewis, he'd send her away to work on some other project for him. He had firms in other major cities. She didn't need to limit her expertise only to restoration projects.

Turning from sulky contemplation of the licking red-blue flames of the fire, she glanced up at the same moment Marion entered the room on the arm of Mitchell Newmann.

Marion's tiny head was thrown back as she peered up at her new guest. A look almost of rapture was visible on her face while she listened intently to his low, privately-spoken words. A gurgle of laughter burst from her lips and she patted his muscular arm threaded around her slight one.

Brittany's eyes flew to meet the humor-sated ones of the tall man whose forceful presence seemed to fill the room. He didn't appear to be startled to see her.

"Come meet our other friend, Mr. Newmann."

"Please, Mrs. Stanford, call me Mitchell." His deeply vibrant voice was toe-curling in its masculine appeal, and Marion responded positively.

"I'll do that, my dear, if you'll call me Marion." She twinkled up at him, drawing him into the room toward the waiting trio. "You know my husband, of course, so I'll skip him and introduce you to one of his brilliant young associates, Douglas Kennedy."

Brittany watched with rapidly increasing pulse while the two men shook hands and made a swift measuring appraisal of each other. Then, the enigmatic grey eyes were turned on her, and she heard Mitch say, "Nice to see you again, Miss Lawson. I understand you're here to celebrate tonight."

His hand was red-hot on hers and she knew her own

must be like icicles. Her smile felt frozen, too, her entire face stiff, but somehow she had to speak. "Yes, and I really should thank you, since you made the evening possible through your purchase of the Casebolt House."

"Your gratitude must be entirely to Lewis Stanford and his excellent reputation throughout the country." His eyes were blank chips of granite, his voice, dead wood.

Lewis came forward to shake hands and give a modest disclaimer. "If my name means anything at all, it's due to the inspired work of an unbeatable network of young associates like Douglas and Brittany. If Marion and I had our way, they'd have the name of Stanford. We love them like they were our own." His hazel-green eyes moved tenderly from one to the other, making his words more than mere platitudes. "Something to drink?"

"Ginger ale is fine. I envy you, sir. Such unusually close relationships must make your work seem more like recreation. I've found more than one week of my job drag by with rather dreary repugnance. Several times in the past few years, I've seriously considered giving it up."

The melancholy in Mitch's emotion-roughened voice was alarming, and Brittany struggled to repress the surge of sympathy she felt for him.

"It's a good thing you didn't, sir," Doug said, shaking his head in awe of the man he admired. "There are several great cities in this country of ours that owe their survival to your genius."

Mitch turned to regard him after tasting his soft drink. "Ten years ago—even five years ago—I had your same enthusiasm for my projects. Don't get me wrong, I still believe strongly in what I try to do to revitalize the inner cities. It's gratifying work; but, I finally realize there's more to life than fulfilling career goals. I want to spend quality time with my family before it's too late."

"My opinion of you went up a giant leap with that statement, Mitchell." Marion patted the place next to her on the couch. "I'm a firm believer in putting priorities in the right order of importance. Your wife must be thrilled with your decision. Did she help you choose Casebolt House for your home in San Francisco?"

Mitchell sat forward, after placing his glass on the low table in front of him, and with his elbows supported by his knees, slowly rubbed the palms of his hands together. His eyes never lifted from a pensive contemplation of the activity. He was silent for so long that Brittany could hear the snapping from the logs in the fire and grew angry with them for disturbing her concentration on his answer. When it came, it was barely audible.

"No, she didn't, but I know she would have approved. I am, unfortunately . . . a widower."

The impact from that one hesitantly-spoken word sent Brittany reeling. She pressed back a gasp with the shaking fingers of one hand. With the other hand she hung for dear life onto her glass of water. The blood seemed to be draining away from her body. *When? How? Why didn't he tell me today?*

Marion was speaking again. Thank goodness, she knew how to handle situations like this. "Oh, my dear man, I didn't know. Forgive me for my thoughtless questions."

"There's nothing to forgive, Marion. You had no way of knowing. I don't talk about it to anyone because it happened quite some time ago."

"Then it wasn't a recent tragedy for you. I'm glad about that. We never forget those dear family or friends we lose when death takes them from us, but the pain we suffer diminishes with the healing grace of God and the passage of time. You must have children, then, Mitchell. You said you planned to have your family with you."

Mitch's smile was fleeting. "Yes, I have a daughter. She's been with my mother in Denver since she was five, when my wife died. I've been on the move too much since then to have her with me, but I want her to know me better before she gets any older. Thirteen is an age of growing independence. My mother feels she needs someone around with greater authority now, and I agree. That's why I accepted the long-term project offered me here."

While Brittany listened to his shocking words with one ear, her mind was doing some rapid arithmetic. Five from thirteen equalled eight. *Eight years!* The glass slipped from her fingers and crashed with finality onto the hearth, splattering a thousand minute slivers of crystal.

"Brit! Are you all right?" Doug leapt to her side and drew her away from the danger of the shattered goblet. "Can you feel any glass in your legs or feet? Here, sit down and let's check." Marion jumped up to vacate her chair, and Doug kneeled to examine her for injury.

"I'm fine, really. Don't fuss, Doug." She pushed him away with an overly bright smile, conscious of the worried looks on the faces of the Stanfords as they clustered around her. "I'm embarrassed at my clumsiness, Miss Marion. Please, forgive me. I don't know how it happened."

"Oh, my dear, don't apologize about anything. We're only concerned about you. You didn't get injured by flying glass?" Her fragile fingers reached out to smooth the hair from Brit's face and paused to press against her forehead. "Do you have a fever, Brittany? I didn't think you were quite like yourself tonight. You seemed rather high-strung and nervous. Are you coming down with something? Has Lewis been working you too hard?"

"No, no, of course not." Brit pushed herself out of the chair with supreme effort. She simply couldn't let

41

her friends think her unheard-of behavior was due to illness or something they had been responsible for bringing about. "I'm not ill, Miss Marion, and Lewis couldn't possibly overwork me. I guess I shouldn't have stayed so close to the fire. It made me warm and much too relaxed. I will feel forgiven if you'll let me get a broom and clean up this mess before dinner."

"I have a better idea," Lewis declared, putting his arm around her shoulders and walking her toward the dining room. "We will all go in to enjoy that dinner right now. I'm feeling rather ravenous, if the truth were known. Mrs. Chang will take care of the cleaning up." As they entered the candle-lit room, he leaned toward her and squeezed her shoulder. "Are you going to be all right, honey? You seem so nervous."

Brittany nodded vigorously, not trusting the steadiness of her voice.

"Everything's going to work out. You'll see. This is your year to shine, and we're going to help you make it happen."

Sliding onto the chair he pulled out for her at the table, Brit heaved a sigh and steadied her upper lip before peering up at him. "Have you added mind reading to your list of talents?"

"Those expressive dark eyes of yours talk, honey. You haven't learned to hide your feelings yet." He dropped a kiss onto her cheek, and turned to greet the others as they entered the room. "I hope you young men have brought your appetites with you, because Marion and Wong, our cook, have put together a Chinese meal to rival any served at the best restaurants in Chinatown. Mitchell, if you will help my lovely wife with her chair, I'm going to put you to her right. Douglas, if you will take the place next to our guest of honor, you can congratulate yourself on having the only position between two of the most charming women I've ever met, bar none."

42

Brittany spread her napkin onto her lap and made a special effort to catch Marion's eyes and smile at her. With three dear friends surrounding her at the table, she should have all the physical and moral support needed to get through the meal. None of them knew that Mitchell's quiet revelation had torn open an old wound, that the pain was so excruciating she could scarcely breathe, let alone talk. They would never know, if she could help it. Nor would Mitchell! How he must hate her—a woman who seemingly couldn't love a man with a motherless child to support.

Perhaps if she told him. . . . No, it was far too late for explanations. She had refused to seek them from him, and he wouldn't accept any of hers, now. He wanted nothing more to do with her, and she had suffered enough already. The pain had been slow torture, like pulling off a bandage from her arm one hair at a time. But she had deserved it. She had been an immature, terrible fool. Mitch was a *widower!* Why didn't I trust him enough to know he could never cheat on a wife, or leave a child? Why didn't I seek to learn more about his past, his outside interests? Why didn't I known a man his age would have experienced a married life? I was so blind to reality . . . so very much in love. He was so immensely careful during the slow growth of our relationship. A perfect gentleman.

A wave of self-pity swept over Brittany, and she mentally trampled on it, replacing it with a watered-down version of what had once been an innate sense of self-preservation. Somehow, she had to carry on with things as they were. She had ruined her relationship with Mitchell because of a hasty decision; she couldn't ruin Lewis's reputation, now, by walking out on a project likely to bring even greater recognition to what he was trying to accomplish in his final years of life. She couldn't ruin Doug's opportunity to seek a job on Mitch's latest development. She couldn't ruin Miss Marion's beautifully prepared dinner and evening of celebration.

43

Sighing deeply, Brit sipped from her water goblet. She would continue with the charade she had established when arriving in San Francisco—that of a dedicated, energetic, eager-to-succeed career girl, with no place in her life for a man. It was her only alternative.

Fixing the semblance of a smile on her face, she raised her heavy black lashes and met the slate grey gaze of the man across the flickering candle flames.

"Prepare to enjoy the most divine meal this side of heaven, Mr. Newmann," she said lightly, grateful that the dinner was in progress before she had to address him. "If my sense of smell isn't deceiving me, we're about to begin with Wong's velvety smooth asparagus soup, and proceed with Peking duck. It consists of delicious, almost-lacquered, crackly skin wrapped with scallions and hoisin sauce in crepe-thin pancakes. Mmm, am I right, Miss Marion? Have you ordered Wong to serve all my favorites tonight?"

"Indeed, I have, dear. Lewis and I want this day to be one you will never forget, from beginning to end. My small contribution toward the making of this special memory is to provide the finishing touch—your favorite dinner. Wong is thrilled over the opportunity to do the actual cooking."

Brittany laughed mirthlessly to herself. Marion didn't know it *was* a day to remember forever—as the *darkest* day in her life—the day she learned her suffering had been needless—the day she learned she had lost Mitchell Newmann because of her own judgmental stupidity.

Suddenly, it was too difficult to pretend indifference for Mitch's sake. What he thought of her was important, but not any more than the love of her dear friends. Brittany swallowed the enormous lump in her throat and blinked furiously to stem the rapid accumulation of tears. "You're too good to me, all of you. I don't deserve it." She tried to push back the rush of

44

intense emotion threatening to put her in a tailspin. "You know how premature this celebration is, I hope," she continued, attempting a tremulous smile. "I haven't done a minute's work on the Casebolt House yet, and I might fail, miserably. Maybe you should have waited."

Doug Kennedy chuckled and put down his soup spoon. "Now if that isn't a switch. Brit, gal, you're always trying to make tough decisions, always declaring you can do things by yourself. She got her big golden opportunity today, Lewis, and now what she really wants to do is rub it in, any way she can . . . even resorting to this incredibly maudlin performance. Go ahead, Miss Lawson, I can take it. I don't mind being left behind while your fame spreads, but you don't have to rub my face in your dust!"

Grasping at Doug's miraculously propitious sense of humor, Brittany laughed overly hard and teased him back. "He's jealous! Don't worry, dear heart, I won't forget you."

"Perhaps I can do something to help you achieve your own measure of fame, if that's what you want, Kennedy." Mitch's deep, authoritative voice cut through the jocularity with cool incisiveness. Immediately, the room was plunged into a hushed silence. Every eye at the table was focused on him. He met Brittany's startled gaze with a steady look that betrayed no hint of his feelings for her.

"One of the reasons I'm making a new home in San Francisco is the long-term commercial venture I've contracted to oversee. Although I take an active role in the initial plans of my undertakings, I like to use local architects for the actual renderings. I don't know what your specialties are, Kennedy, but if you're interested in an effort to turn a twenty-one acre former skid row and industrial area into a complex of marketplace-festival facilities, then I'd be happy to look over your portfolio."

45

"Interested!" The word exploded from Doug's lips. "I'd give an arm and a leg to work with you, sir!"

Lewis laughed outright. "There you are, Marion. Now your evening is a resounding success. Both our youngsters are embarking on the road to architectural fortune." He inclined his head toward his equally famous cohort. "You'll be impressed with Doug's designs, Mitchell. He has a little of your touch of genius, and he knows this city's tastes and needs like the back of his hand."

"Good. I'll call your office in the morning and set up an appointment." Mitch's disturbing eyes moved from one face to the other—assessing their reactions perhaps, but containing something more intense—and finally came to rest on Brittany's. "May this day mark the beginning of a new and lasting relationship between the houses of Newmann and Stanford," he proposed solemnly.

Brittany held her glass of water to her trembling lips and sipped slowly. She quickly lowered her lashes to shield her smarting eyes from his penetrating gaze. Had he meant to include her as a member of the Stanford house? Did she dare to hope he could understand her error in believing his wife alive? Could they salvage any of the deep feelings they once had for each other? *Lord, tell me what to do. How should I handle this continued pain and the deep despair it causes? I feel so helpless against the strength of my love for this man!*

The magnetism of Mitch's presence pulled her fearful eyes to his once again, and she searched the rugged lines of his face for even a hint of softening toward her. His face was almost too carefully schooled, but out of the depths of her miserable guilt, she was certain she could feel the hot brand of his reproach. She had rejected him once too often.

Frightened by the intensity of her reaction, she summoned another surge of self-preservation. Dragging her eyes away, she concentrated on finishing the excellent main course of scallops with broccoli and black mushrooms. She could never throw herself at Mitch. She had too much pride.

From the corners of her eyes, she saw Lewis lean toward her. She met him halfway. "Sometimes, if the front door is locked against you, you can sneak in the back way," he whispered.

CHAPTER 3

THOROUGHLY DISGUSTED WITH HER INABILITY to sleep, Brittany surrendered in her tussle with the bed covers and sat up to snap on the small table lamp. She stared bleakly at the clock and reached out to turn off the alarm. Obviously, it wouldn't be needed.

Five o'clock was too early for anything! The newspaper wouldn't arrive for another hour. No morning news show on television began before six. She wasn't in the least bit hungry: that left out eating. Since she hadn't returned to the office after visiting Casebolt House, she was without her briefcase of work. Why hadn't she asked Donna to take it to her car along with her purchases? Oh well, she didn't have an ounce of energy to do anything constructive anyway.

The next time Brit looked at the clock, it was only five-fifteen. What a waste. Lying around moping, disrupting a much-needed night of sleep with a rehashing of past mistakes was an exercise in futility, and one in which no self-respecting, intelligent woman should indulge. She had loved and lost. It was an age-old story shared by many. It was now time to pick up the pieces of her heart and get on with her life.

Throwing her pillow aside, Brittany leapt from her bed and stalked from the gloom of the dimly lit room into the dark hall, and by some innate sense of direction, into a Pullman-sized kitchen. There, she reached blindly for the wall switch, and flicked it on.

Brittany's eyes adjusted to the light, and then, moving swiftly and smoothly, she took the electric coffee pot to the sink. She washed it out, refilled it with fresh water and then reached for the can of coffee on the shelf next to the stove. Usually she lessened the amount of crystals by half according to the recommended recipe; today, she used the full amount. She wanted her coffee strong and she needed all the stimulation caffeine provided.

Standing with her hands on her hips, Brittany bit at the skin on the inside of her lips. Okay, Step One of PROJECT POSITIVE ACTION had been accomplished. The coffee was perking. *Now what?*

Looking down at her bare feet on the cold linoleum floor, Brittany wiggled her toes impatiently. Step Two was self-explanatory. A determined woman of action should be properly attired. Bare feet and slinky peacock-blue silk pajamas were hardly conducive to the activities she had in mind.

Concentrating only on taking an efficient shower, on getting her heavy mass of hair shampooed and dried, and on dressing in a comfortable work outfit, Brittany accomplished her next goal in record time.

It was only five-forty-five! Allowing herself one quick mental groan, she reminded herself that she had a long, *long* way to go before saying goodbye to another workday.

Applying her make-up with slightly more care than usual in order to cover the tell-tale signs of her sleepless night, she stepped back from the mirror to check the final results. Not bad. The coverstick had done its job well, and the miracle of artfully-applied powder blush gave her the look of a woman in glowing good health.

Tucking the sides of her hair behind her ears with two combs sporting brass leaves, she turned her head from side to side to judge the effect. A smart working gal always fixed her hair in a way that was not only easy to tend, but also not distracting. But, being *practical* didn't have to preclude *attractive*.

Who was she trying to kid? This was not going to be one more normal work day calling for a typically comfortable, serviceable outfit, and suitable make-up and hair care. No. This particular day needed THE WORKS: a carefully coordinated, well-fitting outfit that was suggestive, but not sexy; sporty, but decidedly feminine, and of excellent quality and good taste. It included perfectly applied make-up that enhanced her good features and camouflaged others, and a hairdo that literally became the crowning touch.

Preening in front of a full-length mirror, Brit's eyes traced the lines of another of her new purchases. A fitted long-sleeved blouse of handkerchief-soft, woven linen was primly buttoned and tucked into matching slacks. The Electric Amber color was stunning.

Brit slipped her feet into low, kid-skin heels in a lovely shade of rust, and took one last look before pulling open a vanity drawer to find the finishing touches—three wide brass bracelets worn together on one arm, and a glowing, chunky brass necklace sporting five aspen leaves. They were the fashion rage, and bold enough to catch the eye of the beholder . . . and keep it. Only time would tell if such a ruse worked.

Striding back to the kitchen with more confidence, Brit reached for a mug to hold the freshly-brewed coffee. She smiled wryly at the message emblazoned under its glaze: *A Woman Needs A Man Like A Fish Needs A Bicycle.* She had bought the mug soon after her arrival in San Francisco, and it had served its purpose at the time. She might not *need* a man now, but she *wanted* Mitchell Newmann. There was an empty corner in her life, in her peace-of-mind, in her degree of happiness, that only he could fill. She had never been able to forget him.

Brit refilled the mug and carried it into her living room, snapping on the television as she passed it. Immediately, the test pattern of one of the network stations burst onto the screen. Checking her watch, she saw it wasn't quite six o'clock. Lewis rarely got to the office before eight. What in the world could she do for two hours?

Slumping onto the couch, she propped her long legs up with the footstool. While sipping the hot coffee, she stared at the color pattern on the television screen and gave in to the overwhelming urge to relive the previous day one more time. She forced herself to be more analytical and realistic about her feelings this time, and soon decided there were only three ways the situation could be handled.

She could run away again. Lewis would give her an out-of-city assignment if she insisted on it. It was a weak and ineffective solution, however. Several years and the length of the entire country hadn't enabled her to forget Mitch yet.

She could stay and restore Casebolt House. Maybe the frequent contact with him, and the continual reminders that he no longer cared for her would work him out of her system for good. But, knowing the strength of her feelings, such a scheme seemed highly unlikely and rather sadistic. She hadn't the stamina for daily punishment.

She could go all out and try to win back his love.

Of the three, she preferred the latter solution. Dwelling on Mitch's recent and quite passionate embrace for several more minutes, she convinced herself that his feelings for her weren't completely

51

dead. At least he must have found her physically attractive. She could begin with that. It sounded awfully cold-blooded when put into words, but there was no logical reason why a woman in love shouldn't use every means available to pursue the man of her dreams; and if that included using not only her intelligence, her intuition, her uniquely feminine wiles, but also her physical appeal, so be it. So much for pride.

Gulping the last swallows of her now cold coffee, Brittany sat forward to place the emptied cup on the table, swinging her legs to one side. In the process, she inadvertently knocked two books to the floor. She leaned over to pick them up, and groaned aloud when she saw what they were. "Brit, you're such a dunce! Won't you ever learn?" Relaxing against the couch again, she fingered the soft black binding of her Bible and the five-year diary she had purchased the day Lewis had led her back to the Lord.

Each day in her private devotions—either last thing at night or first thing in the morning, depending on her busy schedule at work—she would first turn in the diary to read her last entry. When her eyes confronted the new blank page, so frighteningly white and devoid of markings, she prayed for God's help in filling it with an accounting of worthy activities and thoughts.

There had been countless days when she had failed, but when facing another new page, she always felt comforted that God in His unlimited mercy and grace had forgiven her past failings. She didn't have to face a single day, a single hour, carrying a heavy load of past mistakes. Or heartaches. Or blazing disappointments. It had taken a long time to learn to lean on God, to accept Him as her lifetime partner, to believe all her tomorrows would be glorious if she walked the high road.

Turning the pages of her Bible, Brittany paused when her eyes fell on an underlined verse in chapter twelve of the book of Second Corinthians. 'And he said unto me, My grace is sufficient for thee: for my strength is made perfect in weakness.''

Lord, why do I always try to make decisions on my own before I consult You? I can't see an inch in front of myself this morning, and yet I'm brazenly plotting a strategy to make someone love me! Imagine that! I spent half the night tossing and turning, unable to sleep a single wink because I felt so unloved, and never once reminded myself that You loved me so much. You died and rose that I might live forever! Now, that's love!

Forgive me for my self-indulgences, and for my shallow faith in Your grace and power, Lord, but life is so complicated. On days like this, I don't understand it at all, and yet here I am, the epitome of a willful, hard-headed Christian, determined to force my will on another, and to make events happen because I want them! What's the matter with me, anyway? Why do I so quickly and so often forget that both Mitch and I are a part of Your plan? That we are both important to You?

What is Your will, Lord? Why is Mitch back in my life? Why have I suddenly learned he is, and was, a widower? Take my hand today and walk with me—no, lead me—each step of the way. Teach me to love Mitch unselfishly, if I must . . . but to wait with more patience than I've ever exhibited for the revealing of Your plan for my life. And Lord, prepare my heart to accept the answer with grace if it's not to my immediate liking!

Satisfied with her decision to leave her future in God's hands, Brittany rose from the couch, punched off the television, and went in search of her camera and a ready supply of film. She would give herself until the completion of Casebolt House. If she hadn't regained Mitch's love and respect by then, she would know it was never meant to be.

As she drove across the city toward Pierce Street, Brit gazed about her with rapt pleasure. She had loved San Francisco from the moment she arrived by plane from the East Coast and reveled in the beauty of the sculptured coastline and golden Bay; but, now that it held the man she loved, it took on an added vibrancy not even the morning fog could dampen. The city soared upward into the early rising sun, surrounding her with the excitement, charm, and history she had come to appreciate with the fierce loyalty and protective eye of a San Francisco native.

With a mounting sense of joy, Brittany drove her three-year-old red Cutlass sedan up the driveway of Casebolt House, and parked near the steps leading to the front veranda. For several minutes, she sat and examined the facade. From a distance it appeared to be quite beautifully preserved. The three-storied house, built in the 1860s, was one of the most formal and elaborate homes of that decade. A passerby from the street would be shocked to discover it had been built of wood and designed in such a way as to simulate rusticated stone. All of the architectural elements were distributed symmetrically around a center entrance and portico, and the formality of such an arrangement was complemented by the equally formal reinforcement of the landscaping. Two huge twin cypresses stood guard on either side of the porch, and closer to the street, a pair of palms added a certain stately appeal.

Leaving the car, Brittany hung her camera around her neck, and took a pen and pad in hand. For the next two hours, she examined every inch of the house, taking notes on her observations. She stopped often to take a Polaroid picture, waiting until the print had fully developed, to be sure it was a good one of each view. Then, armed with notes and the pictorial data of every room, nook, and cranny, she drove to her office to begin the careful plans for the restoration process. Completely engrossed with project ideas that were coming faster than she could fully digest, she breezed into the outer reception office and passed the startled secretaries before they could look up from their work.

"Brittany, wait!" Donna Greene called after her in a loud whisper, leaving her desk to follow on a run.

When the voice connected somewhere in Brit's subconscious, she turned apologetically to see who had spoken. "Sorry, Donna. Good morning. I didn't mean to ignore you. I was somewhere in space, I guess. I've spent the morning at the Casebolt House, and my mind is whirling with ideas." She rolled her dark eyes and made a rueful face.

"That's all right. I only wanted to tell you a client has been waiting in your office for several minutes. I didn't know where you were, or how long you would be gone."

"Good grief, I must be more excited about the new project than I thought! I completely forgot I had an appointment this morning."

"You didn't, actually. He's a drop-in."

"Oh, one of those." Brit grimaced.

"I'd gladly handle this one, if I could. He's beautiful."

Brittany chuckled, and the craters deepened in her cheeks. "You're a hopeless romantic, Donna. You say the same thing about every male on two feet."

The petite brunette peered at Brit through large-framed glasses, and spoke with mock sobriety. "How can you say that? You know very well I've never placed a male under twenty, over fifty, or already married even remotely in the 'beautiful' category." Suddenly, her elfin face broke into a mischievous grin, and she struck a model's pose, fluffing her wiry curls. "Never fear, Miss Lawson, somewhere in this wonderful world, there's a man actively searching for me, and I intend to let him find me very soon."

Brittany laughed aloud, shaking her head in good-natured dismissal of such outlandish banality, and opened the door to her office. She walked into the spacious room, having already pushed both Donna and the waiting client to the back of her mind. Humming *I Left My Heart In San Francisco*, she strode purposefully toward a long table lining the wall to the left of the entrance, and emptied the camera case of the large volume of photographs.

For no good reason, she felt the crawling prickles of awareness and knew *he* was in the room. It hadn't taken a single sound to announce his presence. She still possessed the inner sense that told her when he was near. Brit took her time before turning to acknowledge him, reminding herself to stay cool. In spite of her precautions, when their eyes actually met across the room, the impact of his icy glare almost bowled her over.

"Mitchell!" she gasped, pressing a shaky hand against her chest, and swallowing in pretended fright. "I completely forgot Donna said there was a client waiting. I didn't know it was you. Forgive me, please. Have you been waiting long?"

"About an hour." Not a trace of warmth was evident in his curt reply. His gaze was hard and inscrutable.

"That long? I'm sorry, again. If I'd known you wanted to see me this morning, I'd have come directly here." Brit flashed him a smile—one that always deepened the hollows in her cheeks. She saw his eyes take them in. There had been a time when he couldn't resist planting a kiss in the center of each crater, and the memory of those precious moments quickened her heartbeats. "You'll be happy to know I'm already at work on your lovely new home, Mitch. I went over the entire structure this morning, and have a fairly good idea of what needs to be done. How's that for efficiency?"

Her bracelet trio clanked together as she slid her hands into the seam pockets of her slacks, drawing his eyes as she had first intended in the early morning. She watched his penetrating gaze assess her body. When his eyes returned to her face, she exhibited a breath-holding coyness—or was it panic or wishful thinking—and waited for him to speak. Would he comment on the striking effect of her burnt amber outfit against her copper-toned skin? Did he wonder why she had never married? Did he still find her attractive?

"You always were efficient." He was as aloof and unreadable as he'd been the evening before.

"Yes, well, I learned from a master in the trade. You're quite efficient yourself, you know . . . among other things." She continued to regard him with an openly friendly gaze, meeting his marble-hard eyes steadily. They were both being so careful, side-stepping and using double-talk. She could read between the lines as well as he, and it was obvious they both wanted to avoid a verbal confrontation. Well, good. The longer she could avoid one, the better. Time, and a series of positive judgments regarding her work, might help offset the tragically misinterpreted one separating them.

"I was brought up to believe hard work was good for you. It doesn't hurt, and it gets the job done." There was a bitter edge in Mitch's voice, and a harshness she didn't remember. "Over the years, I've also learned hard work is an effective panacea for . . . for a number of things." He left the window where he had been leaning against the sill, and walked toward her.

Fighting an overwhelming desire to voice her understanding and compassion, Brittany fiddled, instead, with her bracelets. His comments probably referred to the death of his wife, and not to her sudden departure. "Was there something special you wanted to discuss with me this morning, Mitch?" she asked quietly.

He had turned his attention to the photographs on the table, pushing them around with his long, well-groomed fingers. They were the fingers of an artist, expressive and skilled. Beautiful hands. Gentle hands. She wished they would reach out for her now, and hold her, and caress her, and sooth the pain in her heart.

"I came to impress on you the urgency of beginning the renovation as soon as possible," he said stiffly. "My daughter finishes the school year after the first of June. I want her to spend as much of the summer with me as we can arrange." His voice trailed off, waiting for a comment from her. Or was he having difficulty talking about his daughter, still believing Brittany disliked children?

"A month doesn't give me much time."

"Hire a double crew. Work them overtime."

"I'll do my best to accommodate your wishes, but some things can't be rushed. I do have other clients."

"Turn them over to someone else."

"I can't do that. You wouldn't either, under the same circumstances." An element of impatience with his demands slipped into her response, causing him to cast her a sidelong glance.

"You're right," he conceded softly.

Snatching at this first sign of thaw in his cool reserve toward her, Brittany shuffled the photographs around and pushed several away from the others. Her hand accidentally brushed one of his, and she pulled it back quickly, holding it behind her back to hide the trembling. The warmth emanating from his skin had been enough to initiate the remembrance of a galaxy of loving touches.

"I thought the large, sunny room across the hall from the master bedroom would be perfect for your daughter," she said hurriedly, clearing some of the huskiness from her voice with a short cough. "It has a multitude of built-in shelves surrounding a wonderful fireplace. I remember when I was thirteen. I never had enough display space for my collection of books, knick-knacks, and stuffed animals. I plan to enlarge the closet space and make a private entrance into the bathroom next door. A girl on the verge of young womanhood shops endlessly for one more outfit, and appreciates the added privacy and space when she entertains her friends. What do you think? Does it sound like your daughter will like it?"

As she spoke, the enthusiasm she had for the project seeped through unbidden by any ulterior motives of trying to please him, but Mitch was silent for so long, she turned her head to look up at him, her eyes wide and questioning.

He was undemonstrative, seemingly lost in a world of his own. "Mitch?" Brit's low uttering reached through to him, and she watched his lips thin before he arched one heavy brow to throw her a sidelong glance of scarcely disguised impatience.

"I told you once already the entire project was yours, Miss Lawson."

Miss Lawson. He was as hard as old cement. "But, it's for *your* daughter," she pressed.

"You know more about girls and what they like than I do. Whatever you decide is fine."

Brittany raised her voice in protest again. "But I don't know anything about *her!* Not every girl is the same. What are *her* favorite colors? What are *her* hobbies? What is *she* like?"

A muscle tightened in Mitch's jaw. "I don't know!" he rasped, pounding one fist on the table in annoyance. "Stop picking at me with trifling details. Just get the place fixed up into a livable home. You already know what I like. We talked about it often enough." For one brief second, the haunted look in his deep grey eyes showed a familiar vulnerability; but before she could respond to his outburst, he stormed from the office.

Brittany collapsed onto the closest chair. Drat her dastardly weakness for Mitchell Newmann! She hadn't made the least impression on him. Her appearance hadn't attracted his interest at all, and her morning's activity on his house hadn't raised his regard one single iota. This was obviously a one-sided love—hers. She should at least be rejoicing in the knowledge gleaned from his last remark. He hadn't forgotten their long discussions; he remembered they had once shared even the most unimportant and obscure detail of their interests, likes and dislikes.

Every detail but one, she corrected herself sullenly. Mitch had failed to mention he was a widower with a young child.

O Lord, at this moment of discouragement, it seems almost impossible to keep faith. I know there are lots of people who believe the old cliche, 'Never underestimate the powers of a woman in love', but right now I don't think I can even move from this chair. I wish You could just miraculously make another personal appearance, invite Mitch and me out for dinner and tell us what to do, because I don't think I have the ability to play this waiting game. Look at me. I'm a wreck after ten minutes alone with the man. Don't get me wrong. I don't for one minute think I'm so much more special than any other woman in my position that I deserve special favors from You . . . but, maybe I'm the only one who has the nerve to plead for help in rekindling the love of a mortal man!

"Brit?" Douglas Kennedy poked his head around the still-open door of her office. "Was that Newmann rushing out of here? I suppose he already told you I've been hired to work on his new project." He pushed the door wide and came into the room, too intoxicated with the energizing thrill of his newly acquired undertaking to notice her distress.

"Yes, that was Newmann. No, he didn't tell me."
Brit tried to respond to his excitement, but had
difficulty forcing even a thin smile. "Congratulations."

"Is that all you can say, gal? This is the happiest
day of my professional life!" He pulled her up from
the chair and swung her around, laughing as gleefully
as a young boy receiving his first two-wheeled bike.

"Doug, put me down, you crazy loon!" In spite of
herself Brit heard the ring of her laughter. Only Doug
Kennedy would attempt to twirl an Amazon with legs
like flag poles. "Congratulations!" she shouted this
time, all the while clutching his shoulders with a tight
grip.

"That's better, Miss Lawson." Doug stopped the
whirling, but kept his arms around her waist. "I'm
giving a small dinner in my honor tonight to celebrate
my good fortune. Will you come?" His green-flecked
eyes smiled expectantly, and she didn't have the heart
to disappoint him.

"It depends on who else you're inviting, sir," she
teased.

"Other than you, only one outrageously good-look-
ing man—myself. What do you say to dinner at the
Venetian Room of the Fairmont Hotel?"

"My, my, when you celebrate, you celebrate! What
lady in her right mind would turn down an invitation
like that? I'd love it, you nut, but don't choose the
most expensive place in town. I'm so proud of you,
I'd willingly share your good fortune at McDonalds."

"Thanks for those pretty words, but since it's my
party for me, I'll settle for nothing but the best. Put on
your glad rags, and I'll pick you up at eight." For a
moment, he sobered and gazed into her eyes, perhaps
looking for a glimmer of interest beyond that of a
close friendship. Whether he found what he was
looking for or not, he immediately reverted to his
lighthearted charm, dropping a quick kiss onto the

smooth skin of her cheek. "Thanks again, Brit. I'll let you get back to work now. See you tonight."

"I'm looking forward to it, Doug. Thanks for the invitation." She sensed his disappointment in her reaction, and tried to put more feeling into her words. "I'm honored that you want me to mark the occasion with you."

"And well you should be, young lady," he flashed back. "Your date is the new man about town."

"Get out of here, you zany peacock! Save some of that malarkey for someone else." She playfully booted him from her office and closed the door behind him. Was she a fool to spurn his desire for a deeper relationship? A life with him could be satisfying and happy. He made her laugh. They had a great deal in common. It wouldn't be difficult to learn to love him.

Listen to her. That kind of love had all the excitement of an eggnog. A woman's love for her husband should leave her almost breathless with the anticipation of his touch, and somewhat on edge whenever he was away from her. The sound of his voice should bring a thrill of happiness, a mere look from across the room a warm glow of pleasure. She should feel deep contentment in the sharing of her life with him, and yet know an almost continuous dull ache in the depths of her heart over the intensity of her love for him.

There was only one man who fit that description. He wasn't her husband, but she loved him like that now. The thought of his name brought tears to her eyes and an escalation of her pulse. It would be cruel to even attempt substituting Doug for Mitch.

Brit sighed deeply, and walked to the table holding pictures of Casebolt House. Until her dream project was finished, her heart was completely occupied.

CHAPTER 4

AT EIGHT O'CLOCK, Brittany was dressed and waiting in her living room for Doug's arrival. She was literally starving, and her feet were killing her. Two aspirins had successfully dulled a nagging headache, but she was having difficulty keeping her eyes open. She was determined, however, to be vivacious, charming, witty, and attentive for Doug's sake.

When she opened the door to him, she knew she was off to a good beginning. The look on Doug's face said it all quite plainly. "You look ravishing tonight, Brit. If this is how you dress for dates in fancy establishments, I'd better change my tastes permanently." He whistled appreciatively.

"I take it you approve of my dress, Doug," she returned with a curtsy. "You don't think it's too brash?" The dress was one of her favorites—a sensational two-piece outfit in a kaleidoscope of color. The background was tomato red, and it was splashed with royal green, gold, and magenta abstractions—a dress that never failed to perk up her party mood. It had a square-necked top with shoulder tucking, and three-quarter sleeves trimmed in magenta.

"Are you kidding? It's perfect. The few times I get to the Venetian Room, I want everyone there to know it. You'll put us in the spotlight the second we arrive. I hasten to add that's not just due to the dress. It merely enhances your own beauty, and you never looked better. I'm a mighty lucky guy."

"Douglas Kennedy, I believe you've missed your calling. The right words trip from your tongue with such glibness you should be in politics."

They shared laughter again.

"Much as I'd like to keep you to myself, Brit, I'm pretty hyper tonight—exactly the right mood for the glamor and tinsel of San Francisco society in all its glory. Do you mind if we leave right away?"

"Of course not, silly. This is your night and you have the right to celebrate in any manner you choose. I'm the fortunate gal who gets to enjoy it with you. You look pretty special tonight yourself, you know. I don't think I've ever seen you in black tie before. It suits you."

Doug blushed and adjusted the tightness of the stiff collar on his shirt with a finger. "It's not my favorite attire, but I've heard women can't resist a man in a tuxedo. Who knows, after tonight, I might never take it off. Do you think success really does make the man?" He swaggered across the room with one hand in his trouser pocket and struck a pose, stroking an imaginary mustache.

"No, I certainly don't, and you don't either." Brit scowled. "Don't tease about that, Doug. You were already a success before Mitchell Newmann came to town. He didn't commission you because you were a failure and needed a handout to boost your career. He knows he's lucky to find an architect with your talent, and don't you forget it."

"Yes, dear, whatever you say." Doug looked surprised at the unexpected harshness of her outburst. "I'm glad you're on my cheering squad. I didn't know you cared so much." His voice grew soft and the warmth of his smile betrayed his delight.

"Of course I care. I'd be a lousy friend if I didn't." She hated like the dickens to add that last comment, but the instant spark of interest she saw light up his eyes needed a dousing before the evening progressed any further.

Doug didn't miss the message. "Well, you're certainly not that, pal. You're the dearest *friend* I've ever had." He raised one bushy red eyebrow while dropping the other lid in a slow wink. "What do you say we go rub shoulders with the elite patrons of the Venetian Room and show off a little? Are you ready to go?"

"Now you're talking, sir. I'm not only ready, but willing and able. I've never been to the Venetian Room and it has long been on my list of 'must-do' experiences." She tucked her hand through the crook of his arm and darted him a grateful look.

Patting her hand where it lay against the darkness of his tux sleeve, Doug led her toward the door of her apartment. "I'm the guy who's taking you there. On the way you can tell me all about those other 'must-do' experiences of yours. Maybe we can work out some sort of joint venture and systematically cross them off the list."

Brit paused to make sure the door was locked before heading toward the elevator. "That sounds good to me, Doug, but I have a sneaking suspicion our mutual new boss plans to keep us otherwise occupied for the next few months. I'm under strict orders to work double time on Casebolt House. Would you believe Mitch actually ordered me to give up my other clients and hire two shifts of workmen?"

"He must be in a hurry to move in." Doug avoided looking at her and punched the button to head the elevator for the ground floor. "You call him Mitch already. I guess you knew him quite well out in Baltimore, huh?"

65

Kicking herself for the slip of tongue, Brit shrugged offhandedly. She wasn't a liar. Perhaps she could skirt the issue. "About as well as any student could while living in fear that she wouldn't measure up on her first postgraduate assignment. Those of us from the school, who were working on the project at Harborplace, called him Mitch in private. It made him more human, and therefore, fallible. I guess I was remembering that." True, every word.

"There's no reason you shouldn't call him Mitch. You're not a student anymore. I'm sure he won't mind."

They left the elevator and walked down the block to Doug's sports car. Brit felt herself dragging. It had been a long and tedious day trying to arrange for all the work crews she needed, especially since she wanted only the best ones available, those familiar with her and her standards. If she had to watch her conversation all evening and avoid any mention of Mitch, it would be impossible to relax for even one minute.

Mitch Newmann was always on her mind. Now he was on Doug's mind. There would be no peace or reprieve tonight.

Everything changed as soon as she entered the Venetian Room. It was at once beautiful, elegant, and exciting. Following the maître d'hôtel to their table, she saw several well-known personages whose pictures graced both the local newspapers and television screens. She poked Doug when they inched past San Francisco's famous mayor as she rose from her table to leave the restaurant.

Doug stopped to greet her. "Hello, Your Mayorship." His disarming grin caught her attention, and she extended her hand. "I'm Douglas Kennedy, an architect with the Lewis Stanford firm. I'd like to congratulate you on the fine job you're doing for the citizens of this city. I'm especially pleased with the

66

support you showed in the Pier 39 waterfront development."

If the mayor was shocked at his audacity, she recovered quickly enough to smile graciously. "Thank you, Mr. Kennedy. I appreciate your vote of confidence."

Brittany cast a quick look around her, but the other diners were apparently accustomed to such things, and weren't paying the least bit of attention. She slid onto the chair held for her by the maitre d', and waited until he had seated Doug.

When they were left alone, Brit propped her elbows on the table and rested her chin in the cradle made by her folded hands. She watched Doug make a slow perusal of the room, and when he finally met her amused gaze, she laughed silently and shook her head.

"Honestly, Mr. Kennedy, if I had known I would be dining with such a celebrity, I would have worn my tiara. I feel rather plain and ordinary suddenly. Would you mind telling me what got into you back there! How did you dare speak to her?"

"Who?"

"You know who. The mayor!"

"Oh, her. I was merely exercising good citizenship, Miss Lawson. I don't always have access to the good woman. There we were, eyeball to eyeball, and I could tell she was dying to know who I was. It seemed rude to snub her."

A ripple of laughter broke from Brittany's throat. "Oh, Doug, you're too much!"

"Did you see how her eyes lit up when I dropped that compliment on her?"

"I'm afraid this is going to be a long summer. If your new job has swelled your head this much in one day, you're going to be unbearable by fall."

"I don't know how you can say that, Miss Lawson. I'm beginning to feel I was born to hobnob with the rich and famous. How about you? Could you get used to this life?" Doug surveyed the elegant room with relish.

"I'd be crazy if I said no, but if I'm allowed to give you a straight answer in the midst of all this zaniness, I would have to say it would depend on the person with whom I shared it."

"How about your present company?"

"I always enjoy being with you, Doug. You make me laugh."

"That's not what I was talking about, friend."

"I know."

In an attempt to steer them toward safer topics, Brit inspected the dimly lit dining room and its patrons. "A room like this makes everyone look glamorous, doesn't it? The musicians are playing my favorite dreamy music."

Without warning, her eyes locked with those of a familiar slate grey. Even from across a crowded room Mitch Newmann was a force to reckon with. His cynical eyes burned her from head to foot, and she could feel a flush of discomposure rise from the back of her neck. Why was he looking at her like that? She was free to date Doug if she chose. Who was he with and why?

Tearing her gaze away, she sought the orchestra as a diversion in a feeble attempt to get her thoughts under control. She wouldn't let Mitch's presence ruin her evening with Doug. Why had he chosen the Venetian Room tonight? Had Doug informed him of his plans? Listen to her foolishness. As though Mitch cared one way or the other. He would never follow her. He was too mature and busy for such shenanigans.

Unwillingly, she allowed her gaze to drift to him again. He was by far the most distinguished looking man in the room. He had always been devastating in evening clothes. Of course, even in casual slacks and cotton shirts, he managed to look trim, and masculine. It wasn't important, his appearance, but when packaged together with his keen intelligence, his self-assurance, his remarkable talent . . .

"Hey, dreamer, remember me?" Doug tapped her hand. "Who are you staring at? Is he better looking than me?"

"Sorry, Doug. I caught a glimpse of our famous new boss and got carried away wondering why he's here and who's with him at the table."

"Newmann is here?"

"Yes, a few tables to your left."

"How about that. Think we should go over and speak with him?" Doug craned his neck to locate the object of their discussion. "Maybe we should invite him over."

"No! I mean, it looks like he's pretty busy, and it's more fun keeping our celebration private, don't you think?" Brit reached out to touch his hand, and when he gave her a quizzical look, she smiled flirtatiously.

"Perhaps you're right. The way you look tonight, he'd have a hard time resisting you, and I have a feeling I'm no match for the suave Mr. Newmann." Doug covered her hand with his free one and squeezed it affectionately. "When you smile at me like that, Brit, I feel about ten feet tall."

"My goodness, Doug, you are absolutely spoiling me with compliments tonight. If I stop smiling long enough to have another look at this fantastic menu, will you resume your normal size so that we can talk about your new project?"

Doug laughed and brought her hand to his lips, pressing an ardent kiss onto her fingertips.

"Is this little tête-a-tête too private for me to interrupt?"

Brittany snatched her hand from Doug's lips. A buzzing in her ears almost drowned Doug's reply.

"Not at all, sir." He rose to shake hands with

69

Mitch Newmann, who had loomed over them suddenly. "Glad you stopped by. Actually, we're celebrating our good fortune in landing commissions with you and your company."

"I see. I'm glad you feel that way. I feel pretty fortunate myself."

Hearing the unusually solemn timbre in Mitch's voice, Brit abandoned her intention to ignore him, and sneaked a peek through the thick curtain of her half-raised lashes. He was so tall, it was necessary to lift her chin. By the time her eyes reached his face, he was waiting for her.

"Good evening, Miss Lawson."

Immediately, she felt herself drowning in the depths of his pearl-gray eyes. She tried to answer with the same degree of nonchalance, but had to settle for a ghost of a smile. Her tongue was tied in knots. It was inane, and totally contrary to her philosophy regarding male-female relationships, to continue behaving like a ninny whenever Mitch was within her sight.

Fighting for a quick recovery of poise, she purposely sought his attention with her most engaging smile. "Sampling a bit of San Francisco's night life, Mr. Newmann?"

His disturbing eyes appraised her for interminable seconds before a subtle twitching at the side of his mouth betrayed his amusement. He knew her too well. "In a way, Miss Lawson. I was hosting a celebration of my own."

"Oh? And was your celebration too private for *us* to inquire about?" She mimicked his question, and flashed her deepest dimples.

"Not at all. It will probably make the papers tomorrow, anyway. Today, I became a very happy man. I have finally . . ."

"Here you are, Mitchell darling. When I reached the exit, I discovered you weren't behind me."

A sharp pain pierced Brittany's heart. She was too late.

"Sorry. I stopped to greet these folks. This is Douglas Kennedy and Brittany Lawson, both architects from the Lewis Stanford firm. I've hired Miss Lawson to restore Casebolt House, and Kennedy to help design the redevelopment project. May I introduce Alexis Seifert."

Brittany's eyes zeroed in on Mitch's hand where it rested on the waistline of the well-endowed woman who owned the sultry, possessive voice. With both reluctance and morbid curiosity, she lifted her eyes to acknowledge the introduction and to inspect the woman.

She was close to being a classic beauty . . . or would have been, had she been a decade younger. She was doing her best to prolong the look of youth: her make-up was expertly applied, and a professional dying had returned her hair to its original platinum blond. Her bottom lip was a trifle too large, though, and if she continued to pull it down in the corners as she was doing now, there would soon be permanent lines. Her ice-blue dress had probably been chosen to complement her eyes and titillate her escort, but all the sequins and the ludicrously low neckline were rather tasteless on an older woman.

Her command of social amenities couldn't be faulted, however—at least with men. She was turning on excessive charm for poor Doug, and he was falling for it—hook, line and sinker. The woman was obviously a socialite of long standing, and either well-to-do, or the object of a wealthy benefactor. Her diamond and sapphire jewelry was spectacular. Was it a gift from Mitch?

The green-eyed monster of envy had taken firm control, and Brittany tore her pain-filled eyes from their catty critique and fastened them on the sculpted planes of Mitch's face. A fine mist obstructed her vision. Blinking rapidly to clear it, she turned her head as though distracted by the people at the next table.

This woman hanging on Mitch's arm must be the real reason he had accepted the San Francisco project. She had made him a very happy man tonight. Mitch was celebrating his engagement, and the announcement would be in the papers in the morning.

"Brittany? She's struck dumb with your announcement, I guess, Mr. Newmann. Of course, it's not every day we have the opportunity to meet the new owner of a professional football team, especially when that team has recently won the Super Bowl championship, and it's our very own team. No wonder you're out celebrating."

Doug's voice seeped through to Brittany's numb brain and blur of despondency. "Wh-what were you saying, Doug?" She touched her cheek with the shaking fingers of one hand and turned an almost glassy expression in his direction.

He chuckled, and slapped Mitch on the shoulder. "What did I tell you? She's in awe of your prestige and future notability; either that, or she has no idea of the significance of buying the San Francisco Forty-Niners."

"Let me get this straight," Brit continued, feeling the galloping rush of adrenaline as it coursed through her veins at break-neck speed. "You've been celebrating the p-purchase of a *football team?*" Her low, husky voice broke and she fought the impulse to laugh hysterically . . . from the helplessness of her relief.

"That's what I said, Miss Lawson. What did you think I was celebrating?" Mitch's voice reflected his amusement at her confusion. His eyes sparkled, and a myriad of fine laugh lines appeared at each corner.

Brit felt a wave of anger, followed by one of desire for revenge, followed immediately by one of overwhelming jubilation. "I couldn't believe my ears, that's all, Mitch," she gushed, meeting his mocking look with one of her own. "I didn't know you had such an intense interest in the sport. My heartfelt congratulations, and best wishes for many more years of championships."

Sipping from her icy water goblet, her mouth formed a half-smile, and finally a giggle escaped. "Listen to me," she cooed, looking directly into Alexis Seifert's haughty face. "If the truth were known, I'm sick with jealousy. Football is my absolutely favorite sport, and I've grown into an almost fanatical fan of the Forty-Niners since coming to live in this marvelous city." She heard Doug choke on a gasp of incredulity, but went on, caught up in her disgraceful act.

"Here I am, not only toasting the new owner of the team, but realizing I'll be seeing a great deal more of him while working on the restoration of his beautiful home. It's mind-boggling, isn't it? I suppose you're an *old* owner of the team also?"

"No, Miss Lawson, I'm sorry to say I'm not." Alexis peered up at Mitch with an intimate smile that implied it didn't make any difference since she knew the present one so very well.

"Alexis is a lifelong resident of the City." Mitch was duty-bound to come to her support. "Her family has been among the most active in promoting the strong tradition of preservation here. She's the present chairman of the Save San Francisco Bay Association which claims over 20,000 members. As you must know, they were responsible for the development of the San Francisco Bay Conservation and Development Commission which has the final say over my project, and any others like it within one hundred feet of the shoreline."

Brit felt uncomfortable. She had not only put her foot in her mouth, but the whole shoe as well. Actually, she felt downright depressed. Couldn't she get through a single twenty-four hour day without ruining her Christian witness? *Forgive me, Lord. I'm not hopeless. Really, Please hang in there.*

"No, I didn't know, Mitch. I'm an admirer and supporter of the work your organization does, Alexis. I've worked with several of your members in the past. They're great."

"Thank you, Miss Lawson. We don't need any accolades other than the knowledge we're preserving our city for its citizens and their heirs, but it's always nice to hear a word or two of appreciation."

Her rather smug reply and accompanying smile were meant to put Brittany in her proper place as a newcomer of unproven worth. If the men were aware of the subtle battle line drawn by the two ladies, they gave no indication, but Brit felt the hair on her arms stand on end, and was hard-pressed to keep a grip on her tongue. She was not only insanely jealous of Alexis' association with Mitch, but deeply affected by the sight of his arm around her, suggesting both physical and moral support. She managed a rather insipid smile, and returned her gaze to a bleak study of the tablecloth. How long did Mitch intend to hang around? He had flaunted his beloved socialite long enough.

"We'd better be on our way, Mitchell, dear." Alexis took over and finished the untimely meeting with grace and charm. "It was lovely meeting you both, and I wish you nothing but the greatest success on your new projects. Perhaps we'll have the opportunity to meet again soon."

Brittany nodded a reluctant acquiescence, and watched Doug shake hands with Mitch again. He bent over Alexis' fingers. "It was a great honor to meet you, Alexis," he said suavely.

Brit felt a paralyzing pain on her shoulder, and snapped up her head. Mitch held the hard grip until she met his gaze. "I'll see you sometime tomorrow, Miss Lawson." The steel in his voice promised the meeting would not be pleasant.

"Fine," she said, staring back with dark eyes as blank as those on a child's teddy bear.

Doug was silent until the couple was out of earshot. He brushed imaginary crumbs from the table before putting his elbows there, finally leaning forward to peer from under his unruly eyebrows. "Something is going on between you and that guy, and I don't understand it at all. And since when has football been your favorite sport?"

Brittany winced. "Don't even try to understand me tonight, Doug. Haven't you heard that women are a mystery and always will be? The only confession I'll make is that football has always been a mystery to me. I don't really know anything about it, but I aim to become an expert very shortly in case my new boss brings up the subject. That's called 'forewarned is forearmed,' in case you're interested. Let's get on with our celebration, shall we? I'm absolutely famished."

Her confessions were also called deceit, she thought remorsefully, and its implementation was almost always related to the sin of envy.

CHAPTER 5

LATE THE NEXT EVENING, Brittany rose from the drafting table taking up one corner of her home office, and stretched her arms to ease the ache across her shoulders. Except for a scant four hours of sleep the night before, she had worked feverishly on the drawings of the Casebolt House.

Fortunately her first impressions of what needed to be done, and the almost simultaneous vision of how they could be achieved, had worked well on paper. As each detail had fallen into place, her inspiration had grown, making her fingers fly. Naturally she had been reluctant to stop; but, now, seeing the end in sight, she realized how exhausted she was. And hungry.

Actually, she was starving. Since munching on a dry piece of toast around seven that morning, she hadn't even thought of food. Her hand had automatically reached for the coffee pot plugged into the outlet next to her drafting table, but she hadn't stopped for a single Danish to wash down with it. The continuous rumbling from her abdomen was loud enough to be disturbing in bed, and if she wanted to get any peace, she'd need to feed it into submission.

Brit chided herself all the way to the kitchen. Why did she constantly pretend she wasn't interested in food? If she missed a meal now and then, she always made up for the missing calories in the next one. Thank goodness she came from a long line of lanky ancestors. With two hollow legs to fill, she had never had to concern herself with dieting. Of course, she labored hard hours, walked a great deal every day, and worked out for two to three hours every week at a downtown gym. As long as she continued to use up the calories she consumed, she'd be all right.

A quick perusal of the refrigerator whetted her appetite for a substantial meal, and for the moment, her fatigue was forgotten as she became involved in preparing a veritable midnight feast.

With a thick sirloin steak sizzling under the broiler, a pan of refrigerator-style biscuits baking in the oven, and American fries crisp and ready to eat, Brittany used the time remaining to remove her jogging shoes and crew socks. After hours of hunching over the work table, her body was crying out for release from such rigid confinements. With her shirt twisted around her neck like a muffler, she resolved to eat in total comfort by changing clothes.

On the way to her bedroom to switch her cotton knit sweatshirt and shorts for a caftan, she heard the doorbell. Quickly dumping her shoes and socks on the floor, and hastily pushing her arms back into the sleeves of her shirt, she stumbled down the dark hall to the living room. The only light there was the steady red glow of the stereo to indicate it was still on. Guided by that miniscule target and the strains of classical music emanating from its speakers, Brittany made her way across the room to switch on the small wall-hung lamp overhead.

The bell pealed again. Brit took a swift glance at her wristwatch and wondered who in the world would dare to come calling at almost one o'clock in the morning. Leaving the chain attached to the door, she turned the key in the deadbolt lock, and opened the door a scant inch. "Yes? Who's there?"

"Mitch."

"M—Mitch?" Her heart lodged into her throat and got in the way of both her speech and proper breathing. She could feel the rapid escalation of heat invading her body and swore she heard her knees knock. "Wh—what do you want?"

"I have that information you asked for yesterday." His explanation came *sotto voce* through the narrow space, and Brit leaned forward to hear, resting her head against the door. The deep resonance of his voice caused a rapid series of nervous convulsions in her stomach, and she closed her eyes against the painful ache. She had purposefully avoided going to the office in order to miss seeing him after her performance at the Venetian Room. Was he here now to vent his anger at her rudeness to Alexis?

"It's late, Mitch. One in the morning."

"I'm going out of town at seven. I was going to shove a note under your door and noticed your light was still on."

"I've been working."

"I assumed that." There was a hint of both amusement and impatience in Mitch's reply, and Brit felt the stirrings of resentment. Why should he assume she had been working? She could have been entertaining.

"Brit, do you suppose I could come in before we wake up your neighbors?"

A testy objection froze on Brit's lips. This was no time to play hard-to-get. It was a made-to-order situation she should seize with gratitude. Shutting the door, she slipped off the safety chain with shaking fingers. By the time she held the door wide, the mask of an efficient, friendly businesswoman was fixed into place.

"Of course. Sorry." She closed the door and faced his shadowed figure in the semi-darkness of the room.

"It smells like you've been having one of your famous late-night suppers," Mitch said, and his white teeth flashed briefly when his mouth curved upward into a heart-tugging grin.

"Oh, no, my supper!" Brit gasped, rushing past him to the kitchen. Grabbing a pot holder, she pulled open the oven door and took out the pan of biscuits. They were well browned, but salvageable. Shoving the pan onto the stove top, she leaned over to rescue the steak from under the broiler. "Thank goodness! You can't be more than 'medium' and not totally ruined," she crooned, speaking to the spitting hot piece of meat while finding additional room on top the range to place the broiler pan.

"Looks like you haven't cut down on the amount of food you consume, either." Mitch's droll comment came from the doorway.

Brittany shot him a quick glance over her shoulder. "I do tend to over-do, don't I? This is my first meal today . . . yesterday. I'm entitled to every bite of it."

"Smells good."

Was luck going to smile on her this time? Bending again to reclose the broiler door, Brit knew Mitch's eyes would be focused on her long bare legs, and saved any comment on his observation until she had straightened. "There's more than enough for two if you'd like to share with me." She walked casually to a cupboard, as though she didn't care one way or the other, and reached for plates from a shelf a little beyond her fingertips. Raising up on tiptoe, she waited another few seconds before daring to look at him over her shoulder. "Well, how about it. Want some?"

From across the room, his grey eyes looked almost black, they were so deeply set. His imposing figure filled the doorway, and the pale blue of his oxford cloth shirt created a devastating effect against the rich walnut tan of his skin. She was achingly aware of his nearness, and he didn't seem to notice a thing about her.

"I shouldn't impose on you, but the sight of that steak is as irresistible as the aroma. I'm pretty hungry myself. I was tied up with paper work and a late conference, and had to skip supper."

"Stay then. I don't have a dining room, but there are two stools at that counter. Take your pick." Brit smiled to herself while she took down two large dinner plates, and then carried them to the stove with a glad heart.

"If you don't mind, I'd like to wash my hands first." Mitch brushed past her, touching her waist lightly before moving to the sink and rolling up the cuffs of his shirt sleeves.

"Help yourself. There's liquid soap in that container by the hot water faucet and paper towels on that holder above it."

While the water was running, neither of them tried to speak. Brittany busied herself dividing the piece of meat in half, and placing equal portions of the fried potatoes onto each plate. She took a fresh tomato from the refrigerator and sliced it into wedges, adding cottage cheese to form a salad. Scooping the warm biscuits into a wicker basket, she carried it, with a plate of butter, to the narrow counter that served as a table in the miniature kitchen.

"I'm not equipped to serve sit-down meals in this small apartment," she said, feeling the necessity to say something to ease the pounding tension she felt. "If I entertain here at all, I stick to the buffet format."

"The stools and counter are. fine. The food will more than compensate for any discomfort. Can I help with anything?" Mitch regarded her with such unexpected friendliness, she was carried along with it.

"Sure. Get the silverware from that drawer behind you. The steak knives are in the divider to the rear. Napkins are in the next drawer."

Transporting the plates of food from the stove to the make-shift table, Brit couldn't help musing over the domesticity of the scene. She had heard women friends complain about having to cook for their husbands, and she had wondered about the depth of their love. Preparing a meal for Mitch, and sharing it with him over the conversation that usually accompanied the occasion, was high on the list of things she had enjoyed in the past, and greatly missed.

"What do you want to drink, Mitch?"

"Got any milk?" He was right behind her, his hands filled with utensils, and his closeness was overpowering.

"How can you ask that with a straight face?" she retaliated, in pretended outrage. "This is the former milk queen of her 4-H club, remember? Have you ever known me to be without a week's supply of the stuff?" She laughed, and gestured at the refrigerator. "Take your pick, sir. There's chocolate, skim, and good old regular homogenized."

Her eyes followed him hungrily as he went down on his knees in front of the opened refrigerator door. He hadn't really changed. He was still part boy, part man.

"Incredible, the amount of food you consume. You've got pretty good taste, though." He moved several cartons on the top shelf before choosing a new one of skim milk.

"Was that ever in debate?" It was a casual response, but when Mitch straightened, his eyes scrutinized her face for possible double entendre, and she regretted her choice of words.

"I'll let you perform the carton-opening honors," she said hurriedly, having trouble meeting his gaze. "I usually end up with wax in the milk before I get through fiddling with the spout." She left him to the task while reaching for two glasses, moving back to their table with increased awareness of his quiet observation.

For the next few minutes, both of them attacked the meal with rapt attention and enjoyment. There was little conversation. "More milk?" Mitch inquired once, between bites of a biscuit oozing with an excessive amount of butter. His arm brushed against hers, and Brit felt shivers of ice water race through her blood vessels, leaving raised flesh all the way down to her toes.

"Please," she answered, shifting a mouthful of meat into one cheek. Her throat had suddenly constricted, and she knew it would be difficult to swallow another bite of anything. *O Lord, why can't I just tell him I made a mistake and have never stopped loving him? Why do I sit here with sealed lips, fearing he will never believe me? I couldn't bear his rejection. Not yet, Lord. I need more time, more opportunity to hope. Did he suffer any of this agonizing pain when I so cruelly rejected him?*

"This really hits the spot. It's a perfect combination of flavors. I haven't had American fried potatoes for years. Restaurants always make french fries or baked potatoes." Mitch's compliment came as he cleaned his plate of the last crumb.

"Why don't you fix yourself some?"

"I don't have time to do the grocery shopping."

"You need a cook."

"True." He toyed with his glass, watching the milk swirl around the sides. "I need more than a cook, I'm afraid."

Brittany felt the goose-bumps rise further on her bare legs, and wished she had the nerve to volunteer for the job. "What information did you get for me today, Mitch?" Hopefully, he really had some, and wasn't using it as a guise to get at her for her ill-bred treatment of Alexis.

He drained the milk from his glass before answering. "I called my mother yesterday, and she provided the answers to those questions you posed about my daughter."

"Oh, that." Brit reached for the last biscuit and broke it apart. "Want half?"

Mitch's brow arched in surprise at her bland response. "Don't you want it?"

"If I did, I wouldn't offer it to you."

"Not the biscuit. The information."

"Oh. Of course, I do." Brit dabbed at her mouth with a crumpled napkin. "What is your daughter's name, by the way. You've never mentioned it."

"Hally."

"Hally? I don't think I've ever heard that name before."

"It was my . . . her mother's name."

Brittany drew an unsteady breath. "It's very lovely. Tell me about Hally." Why hadn't he continued with his first explanation? Was it so difficult for him to speak of his wife?

"My mother claims her favorite colors are blue and yellow. She said Hally enjoys reading, and has a collection of ceramic and stuffed dogs. She takes piano lessons and picks at a guitar. She's evidently a good swimmer, and is pretty keen about gymnastics. Mother said she had been a cheerleader this year for the junior high football team."

Halfway through Mitch's recitation, Brit turned to stare at him. Before he finished, she was ready to pounce on him. "She sounds absolutely fantastic, and you're spouting the information as though it came from an office memo! Why do you say 'my mother says'? Didn't you know any of these things about Hally yourself?"

"Not really." Mitch piled the dishes and flatware together and carried them to the sink behind them.

"What do you mean by that?" Brit followed him with her eyes, sensing his discomfort but too interested in this hidden aspect of his life to let well enough alone.

"It's none of your business, Brit. You asked me

about my daughter's interests for decorating purposes, and I gave you the information you sought." Leaning against the sink, he thrust his hands into the pockets of his grey dress slacks and jingled coins and keys with noisy aggravation.

"You're giving it to me two days later, and I'm curious, Mitch," she persisted. "If I need to know something more about Hally, will I have to wait for the information until you can call your mother to get it? Don't you know your own daughter, for Pete's sake?"

"How can I?" Mitch defended, a frown creasing his forehead. "I've been on the road for the past several years. I haven't had a home life to offer her. A kid needs stability—roots. She's had that with my mother in Denver."

"A 'kid' needs a parent who loves her enough to take an interest in what she does, and shows his appreciation and pride. *That* can be done across continents, if necessary!"

"I don't need an old maid to tell me how to treat my kid!"

"Thanks a lot. Sounds to me like your kid doesn't need some uncaring, swinging bachelor either. Maybe your mother should put her up for adoption!" Brit pushed back the stool and stood in front of Mitch, running her fingers through her thick jet hair. She was too angry to be put off by his sarcasm. She was hurting. She wanted him to hurt, too. "How often do you go to Denver to see your daughter? More than once a year? What do you talk about when you're together—how busy *you* are? How often do you call her? On her birthday, whether she needs it or not?"

"All this is beside the point, Brittany. I've bought a house now, and if you tend to your business and get it renovated, I'll have Hally living in it soon."

"Hally might be living in it, but she'll hate every minute she spends there if you continue to show as little interest in her as you have so far! A house is not a *home*, Mitchell Newmann! Have you forgotten that?'' Brittany shouted the sharp rebuke. Her hands hugged her hips, her temper completely blew a gasket, and her chest rose and fell with hard, labored aspirations.

She wanted to shake Mitch, and pummel his chest with her fists. Was it only an excuse for her need to touch him? Was it only an ineffective plea for the privilege of helping him provide a real home for Hally?

Mitch's eyes narrowed and seemed to focus on the movement of her lips. She held her breath and stopped the movement altogether, sensing the electricity created by their emotional outbursts. Why, *why* couldn't they both say what was *really* on their minds? Why must they continue to play this game of not caring?

Mitch raised his eyes to observe the rapidly dwindling anger in her dark luminous gaze. ''You're a fine one to tell me how to rear my own daughter,'' he said, his voice husky with feeling. ''You're the self-centered tease who cold-bloodedly played up to me until you discovered I had her, and then walked out without a backward glance. You have the career you put before a family, lady. The only advice I want from you concerns the restoration of my house. My daughter is *my* business.'' He headed through the kitchen door, and into the hallway without a backward glance.

Why had she goaded him again? She simply must learn to think before spouting off! ''Wait, Mitch, it was all a mistake! Let me explain!'' She followed him, her eyes trained on his broad shoulders.

''You already did. Yesterday.''

Halfway through the dimly-lit living room, Brittany caught up with him and pulled on his arm. ''Please, Mitch, don't leave here in anger. I can't work on your

property with all this . . . this *animosity* between us."
She succeeded in stopping him, and waited until he
met her gaze before continuing. "I'm sorry for what I
said. I was out of place. If we can't be f-friends,
Mitch, could we at least be civil to each other?"

She pleaded with her eyes, and his glittered back,
diamond-bright in the muted light. His face looked
almost haggard and a rough growth of beard added
years to his age. Again, she had a glimpse of the
vulnerability he tended to hide behind the facade of a
businessman.

After a long sigh, he rasped, "That's what you want
between us, now Brittany—*civility?*" His hands
reached out to grip her upper arms, and the strength
of his touch sent bolts of intensified longing shooting
up and down her body. "That's asking a lot from
someone who has known you as well as I have."

His fingers tightened on her flesh. "Your eyes still
speak a language of their own, my lovely, dark-haired
gypsy, and they've been talking to me ever since we
met. I've never forgotten those eyes and the messages
they once sent to me." His voice deepened disturbingly, and the gravelly sound assaulted her senses.
"Even now, they're begging me for much, much more
than *'civility.'*"

"Mitch," she whispered, "we have to talk, really
talk."

"You *have* been talking to me, since the minute I
arrived tonight." Mitch's face descended to within an
inch of hers, and his eyes devoured every feature.
"You also flaunted the curves of your lovely long
legs. Well, your little scheme worked like a charm,
Gypsy. I'm only a human being, and not much
different from any other man, except that I have
certain principles that get in the way."

There was a hint of savagery in Mitch's eyes before
his mouth took possession of her already tingling lips.
Brittany ceased her faint-hearted resistance, and

acquiesced with a willing ardor of her own. A pent-up frustration of eons without him was waiting to be slaked. With an outpouring of love, she slid her hands up over his muscled shoulders and held him fiercely against her.

They were together at last, sharing a potentially beautiful portion of life's vitality. But it wasn't enough. And it wasn't at all pleasurable. Not this way.

A small voice somewhere in the distance was trying to warn her, but Brittany was almost beyond listening. Mitch was here. He was holding her, kissing her. Dragging her lips across his whisker-roughened cheek, she cried out in delirious joy, "Oh, Mitch, Mitch *darling*, I love you. *I love you so much!*"

It took a ridiculously long time for her to realize the male shoulders under her restlessly moving hands had turned to stone. She was embracing a cigar-store Indian. "M—Mitch?" she questioned tremulously, feeling the blood pound in her head, and a powerful hand of fear slowly squeeze her heart.

"Is that what you call this, Brit. . .*loving* me? Don't you mean lusting for me? Wanting me?" His gun-metal gray eyes were accusative, and filled with the same revulsion expressed in his bitingly bitter voice. "I almost forgot what kind of person you are." He drew the back of a hand over his eyes. "So help me," he sighed, "I'm not immune to a little lusting of my own, so let's call it by the right name. We're not kids, either one of us, and not without sin, but there's one thing I've resolved to do—I'm saving my *loving* for Hally's next mother."

Brittany's throat was tight and aching. It was difficult to utter a sound. She stood against the wall, groping for an understanding of what had happened, feeling almost disoriented in the shadowed darkness of the room. "You don't understand, Mitch," she said, her voice croaking slightly. "I made a ghastly mistake." A lump swelled and cut off the next words.

"Then we have *two* things in common—our lusting and our mistakes. I'm not about to repeat mine."

Halfway out the door, Mitch paused to add, "I move my family into Casebolt House in five weeks. See that it's ready for us."

Brit managed to remain standing and meet his numbing glare. "I'll do my best, *sir*. Thank you for coming by with the requested data. After this, however, I'd prefer that you call my office and leave any messages with my secretary. I like to keep business affairs separate from my home life. And Mitch," she inserted sweetly, her husky voice trembling only slightly, "you're more than welcome for the dinner."

Only after both the safety chain and the deadbolt lock had been dropped into place behind the closed door did she allow the hot stinging tears to roll unimpeded down her cheeks. It was stupid to cry. She had jumped into a dry pool with both eyes open. Mitch might have broken her heart, but she had provided him the opportunity.

Brit snapped off the small wall light and the stereo, walked lethargically toward the kitchen, and did the same there. The dishes could wait. She entered the bedroom, stepped over the sneakers and socks she had dropped onto the floor in her haste to answer the doorbell, and crawled directly into bed. She didn't even pause to remove the pink shorts and shirt.

Staring at the ceiling in the dark, she pressed her lips tightly to still their persistent quivering. Over and over, she admonished herself: there is no greater fool than a woman in love. She had done this to Mitch. She had ruined his life, caused his bitterness, his hardness, his estrangement from his family. And if that wasn't enough, she had thrown herself at him tonight. Jezebel had nothing on her.

Unable to forgive herself, she turned over and faced the wall, hardening her heart against herself and God.

CHAPTER 6

ARMED WITH A PORTFOLIO OF NOTES, pictures, and architectural drawings, Brittany arrived at the office a few days later, simultaneously with Lewis Stanford. Bleary-eyed from lack of sleep, and unable to change the sullen droop of her mouth, she made no attempt to preface their meeting with light-hearted banter.

"Lewis, I'm glad you're here."

"Getting an early start today, dear?" Lewis moved his eye glasses farther down over the hump on his nose, and peered at her over the rims.

"I was hoping you'd have time to look over a few of my plans for Casebolt House. Mr. Newmann wants part of it restored by early June, but he's totally disinterested in consulting over details. I feel I should have a second opinion before meeting with the foreman at nine o'clock."

"Then we'd better examine them right now. Bring your portfolio into my office. We'll use the display table." He held the door open and watched her precede him into the room. Worry lines creased his forehead. "From the looks of that volume of material,

89

you've been putting in some midnight hours, Brittany. I hope you're not overdoing it." He followed and stood beside her, casting enough sidelong glances to confirm his concern.

"Some," she shrugged, "but no more than usual when I'm busy."

"You look tired, dear. Is your case load too heavy? I'd be glad to reassign some of the work."

"You worry too much, Lewis. I'm fine. If I look a little washed-out this morning, it's because I had insomnia last night."

"Are you worried about something?"

"Not at all. See what you think of my plans for Casebolt House, Lewis. I'd appreciate any suggestions you have to offer." Brit spread out the artist renderings for his perusal, and waited quietly while he read them. When he straightened at last, adjusting his shoulders and back of the kinks acquired from leaning over too long without a break, she regarded him anxiously. "Well? What do you think?"

Lewis put his arm around her waist. "Come and sit with me on the couch, Brittany. Let's talk about it."

"It's that bad, Lewis? I told you I didn't think I was ready to go off on my own yet. I warned you, remember?"

"Sit here, dear." He led her to the sand-colored couch near his desk, and took the cushion next to her, removing his glasses and rubbing his eyes with a knuckle a few times before answering. "I remember what you said, and I also recall my response, Brittany. I stated, categorically, that you were not only well-prepared for the work, but, in my opinion, the best architect in San Francisco for the job. Now, you're calling me a liar."

"Lewis!" Brittany's face paled and she turned startled eyes to meet his stern look. "I would never do that!"

"You already have, my dear, and on more than one occasion these past few days."

"I don't understand. I don't remember."

"I value my reputation in this great city of ours. I've spent thirty-some years building the confidence of the community in work done by this firm. Clients know when I say something, I mean it. They trust me. They know my word is as good as gold." Lewis spoke in his usual quiet, measured tone of voice.

"I know that. I do, too. I wouldn't say anything to . . ."

"Then stop this nonsense about not being capable of restoring Casebolt House. I told Mitchell Newmann you're the best, and I mean it. Those plans of yours are excellent. No, *more* than excellent. They're *brilliant*. Every time you throw out this absurd notion of your inexperience or incapability, you're essentially calling me a liar, and I can't accept that from you."

Brittany blinked her lashes furiously to clear an excess accumulation of moisture from her eyes. Lewis' not-too-gentle tongue-lashing had reached home. Until she had the quivering of her chin under control, she knew it would be senseless to attempt a reply.

"I'm sorry if I'm being too rough on you, but you've got me in a quandary here. Clearly, something is bothering you, and it's of enough significance to affect your health. I don't believe insomnia and anxiety over the quality of your work are the culprits." Lewis paused to fill a pipe with tobacco, and with an alert glance read the pain on Brittany's face. "I'm rather inclined to believe this . . . problem . . . of yours has to do with Mitchell Newmann himself," he added softly. "Am I right?"

Brittany thought of denying it, but quickly changed her mind. Her relationship with Lewis was far too valuable to place in jeopardy with any more lies and deceit, and he had uncanny insight regarding people. On the other hand, she hated to lose his respect, and surely he would find spurned love a ludicrous reason for depression.

"I can see you're not quite ready to confide in me," Lewis continued, taking short puffs from the stem of the pipe he held to one side of his mouth. "Your private life is none of my business, Brittany, and I shouldn't speculate about the tension I notice between you and Newmann whenever you're in the same room. I usually refrain from jumping to conclusions on circumstantial evidence, but you've made it fairly easy for me to fit together a few pieces of the puzzle. You don't have to admit or deny anything, but I'd like you to know what I'm thinking." He stopped to place his pipe in an ashtray.

"I think you fell in love with Newmann out there in Baltimore, and fled to the West Coast, believing he was a married man."

"Lewis, I . . ."

"Let me finish, dear." Lewis patted her knee in silent comforting. "Anger, misunderstandings, and, most assuredly, great distances, can seriously fracture a once close-relationship, but rarely beyond repair. Five years might seem a long, long time to love someone without any returns on the investment, but persistence in the pursuit of true love, as in all things, generally pays off in the end. Keep in mind, Brittany, that if *you* feel like a little unoccupied island—unloved, forgotten, and forlorn—Newmann might, also. Maybe you should be questioning why he's still a single man."

Brittany listened to Lewis' soothing voice, and made no effort to interrupt. Inwardly, she was amazed at how succinctly he could zero in on her problem, analyze it, and come up with the words she most needed to hear. She followed him with her eyes as he rose from the couch and made his way to the table where her work still lay on display.

"I don't profess to know all the answers to life's mysteries," he continued, "but old age does bring with it the wisdom gleaned from more experience.

92

I've known quite a few people in my time who built high barriers against being loved because they felt guilty, or embarrassed, or unworthy. Some of them suffered needlessly all their lives in the mistaken notion they *deserved* the punishment of being unloved, which is nonsense. We *all* make mistakes. Sometimes big ones. What I'm trying to say is, don't be impatient or give up too soon if the mending of what you and Newmann shared is important to you, Brittany. Keep in mind that healing of all kinds takes time. If you come up against a cold wall, don't step back and withhold further affection. Don't call that wall 'rejection' and run, when it might be a wall of self-confinement you're up against. Get a ladder and climb over it! I don't think there's a man alive who can fail to respond to a freely-given wealth of love. . .especially if it comes from a woman as beautiful and fine as you, dear.''

In the silence that followed, Brit rose to join Lewis, placing her arm around his waist in an affectionate hug while resting her dark head against his shoulder. "Thank you for being such a dear friend," she said softly.

"I want you to be happy, Brittany. So does Marion."

"I know. I wish i could talk about it, but I'm not ready to do that."

"If the time ever comes, we're both available any time of the day or night with a listening ear, a broad shoulder, a word of advice or just plain encouragement."

"I'm grateful for your love and support, Lewis, but my personal life is something I must learn to deal with on my own." Brit gathered the materials on the table, stuffing them into the portfolio with reckless haste. Her activity seemed to signal an end to their discussion, and Lewis returned to his desk.

Brittany sensed he was still observing her. The poor

man. She had practically forced him to look over her work, and then had thrown his profuse compliments into the basket. Not only that, out of the kindness of his Christian heart, he had tried to reassure her—to inspire hope for a better future—and she had turned a cold shoulder.

"Lewis Stanford, your only female associate is so despicable. If I were you, I'd throw her out on her ear!" Dropping the portfolio onto the table, she strode toward him with an apologetic grimace, coming round his desk to plant a kiss on his wrinkled cheek. "You should, you know."

Lewis removed his glasses and laugher rumbled in his throat. "Actually I was considering a rather swift kick, *you know where,* but you looked too unhappy."

"Yeah, well, I was a little in the dumps, I guess, but I'm juiced up now, and ready to rebound. I'm no dummy, you know. Without consciously plotting this morning's visit, I knew you would come up with the right medicine. You've never failed me yet." She took one of his hands and held it tightly with both of hers, meeting his close inspection with a tremulous smile. "I'm not going to let you down, Lewis."

"Good. In the process, don't let yourself down either."

"That's always tougher, for some reason. The power of positive thinking isn't all it's cracked up to be. At least mine seems to suffer from a short fuse. One or two minor setbacks, and I find myself back to round one wondering if it's worth the effort."

"That's for you to decide, of course."

"An hour ago, I had decided it wasn't, but now . . ." Brit shrugged and shook her head. "I guess I'm a glutton for punishment." She headed for the door of Lewis' office, stopping to pick up her portfolio and shoulder bag. "Thanks, again," she called, turning to blow him a kiss.

"Any time, dear. My door is always open. Good luck."

For the remainder of the morning, Brittany worked with the contractor overseeing the construction crews. They discussed each phase of the renovation of Casebolt House, and walked over every inch of the house, both inside and out. They pored over her drawings and made several minor changes. Then they concentrated on the rooms that needed to be finished first, making out a temporary schedule of procedure.

It was apparent to them both there was a necessity for either longer work hours, or a double shift of workmen. "I'm concerned that the neighbors won't take kindly to either plan, Mr. Vandervelde. This is a fairly quiet neighborhood. Would it be possible for you to double the number of people working on each crew, and keep to the usual eight-to-five routine?"

"We'll try it, Miss Lawson. We can't have our men stepping on each other's toes, but we won't know if it works until we give it a go. They're all reasonable people, I think. They'll cooperate. We'll spread them out, so many to each room. That way we'll have those five rooms we talked about pretty shipshape by the first of June." Joe Vandervelde grinned at Brit while shifting a cold cigar butt to the side of his mouth. "The owner of this place must be some guy to reckon with. He's asking for a minor miracle."

Brit laughed with him. "That's the truth. He's the new owner of the Forty-Niners, by the way."

"No kidding! Imagine that. I'll have to tell my kid. We try to get to all the games, at least we did last year. Now that they've become Super Bowl champions again in such a short time, I suppose the tickets will go sky high, and we'll have to pick and choose. Say, do you think you could ask this guy for his autograph? My kid would get a real kick out of it— sort of think his old man's okay for once. Billy's birthday is coming up soon."

"Sure, I don't see why not. Mr. Newmann is nice enough." It was time for her to face him again anyway, and asking for an autograph was as good an excuse as any to open communications between them.

She and Joe made plans to meet each day at five-thirty to go over the work accomplished. Joe would be in complete charge of the various crews, as he was on most of the restoration projects for the Stanford firm. It was his responsibility to work directly with the chief carpenter, painter, plumber, electrician, floor finisher, wallpaper hanger, and any other specialists needed, and to orchestrate their activities into perfect harmony. They would, in turn, be responsible for the members of their crews, the quality of their work, and the purchase of supplies needed to accomplish it.

When Joe went off to meet with the crew chiefs, Brittany reshuffled her materials and brought out notes in preparation for her next meeting. Unknown to Lewis Stanford, she had come up with a brilliant idea after their morning discussion, and had stopped at the receptionist's desk to make a phone call.

"Hello-oo." A melodic female voice called a familiar greeting from the living room.

Brit laughed silently and ran a quick tongue over her teeth. "I'm coming," she sang loudly in the same decidedly female method of communication. Hurrying through the breakfast and dining rooms from the kitchen, she entered the reception hall and opened her arms to her dear friend. "Welcome to Casebolt House, Miss Marion."

Marion Stanford hugged her tightly before stepping back to peer at her with flashing sapphire-bright eyes, enhanced more than usual by the glorious blue of her silk sheath dress. "Do you know what you're doing, dear? Are you quite in your right mind this morning?"

"Yes and yes to both your questions. Why shouldn't you be the interior designer for Casebolt House? You've loved it even longer than I have. The idea came to me in a flash, and I knew it was right. We share the same love for these magnificent old Victorian homes; you are an unquestioned expert on every detail of that period of history; and, you still hold a valid license to gain entrance into the designer markets and antique shops.''

''True, but I haven't practiced my trade for many years.''

''You've decorated your own homes, helped dozens of your friends with theirs . . .''

'' *And* I've been a tour guide with the Conservation Society for many years, visiting dozens of our most prominent old homes over the years.'' Marion clasped her hands and rested them against her chin.

''Right. This house needs all your expertise and experience. Together, we'll make an unbeatable team. Mitch has given me carte blanche with the house, and evidently with no set budget for furnishings, although I'll verify that with him again.''

''Mitch?''

Brittany grimaced. ''Mr. Newmann.''

''Go ahead and call him Mitch, dear. I plan to do the same, if he'll allow me the privilege now that I'm an employee of his. I won't charge him for my work, by the way. I don't need the money and it's an honor I shall always cherish.''

''You'll do no such thing, Miss Marion. No professional ever gives her work away. It lowers the value of her worth and ruins it for others needing both the recognition and the money.''

''Then I'll charge him the going rate, and give it all to charity. I have several pet projects that could use a financial boost this year.''

''Now you're talking.'' Brittany linked arms and led her on a tour of the entire house. Marion listened quietly while Brittany explained her plans for each room, and then offered her own suggestions on paint colors, wall paper, and styles of furniture to be purchased. It was mutually decided that only choice pieces should be antiques typical of the late 1800's, while the rest should be of a more eclectic style, enhancing their beauty and value, but bringing modern comfort and usefulness to each room.

When they returned to the living room, Marion's face was bright with inspiration. "My head is fairly buzzing with ideas, Brittany. I'll have to go home immediately to write them all down before I forget. I'll begin tomorrow with paint colors and wallpaper selection, and bring the samples to you for final verification. For some reason, I'm a little nervous about this."

Brittany held her hands and smiled happily. "You must promise me you won't overdo, Miss Marion. Work only on the five designated rooms this month, and if it gets to be too difficult for you, let me know instantly. I can get someone else, you know, but I selfishly wanted the opportunity to work with you on this project. You're going to be wonderful."

"My darling girl, I can't begin to tell you the joy it gives me to hear you say that. It's a lovely thing, when you're old, to have a young person believe you still have something worthwhile to contribute. I'll budget my time wisely, and not overwork. You have my solemn promise."

"Good, because Lewis will fire *me* if I work you too hard. Can I drive you home now?"

"No, no. I have Soo Ling waiting with my car. By the way, will your Mitch's mother be selling her home in Denver, or merely bring the young girl and then visit here awhile?"

Brit saw the gleam of mischief in Marion's eyes as she posed her question. She was too polite to ask for an explanation of the familiar shortening of her employer's name. "Mr. Newmann is not 'my Mitch' and I can't answer your question about his mother. Why do you want to know?"

"If Mrs. Newmann is planning to move here,

perhaps she is also expecting to move some of her furniture. We should know in order to eliminate duplication of pieces, or to keep from making unforgivable errors in decorating taste. Some styles of furniture simply cannot be mixed." The look of horror was so evident on her face, Brittany had to laugh.

"We can't have that, can we? I'll speak with Mit—Mr. Newmann, and find out."

"You do that, dear. Your Mitch will know what to do. Goodbye for now. I'll confer with you sometime tomorrow."

Miss Marion was such a rascal. One slip of the tongue and she had lit up like a candle during a blackout. Her interest was piqued, and now she would slyly work around it until she had all the information at her fingertips.

Brittany returned to the kitchen to get her purse and portfolio. Unless she missed her guess, Lewis was not only in for a shock tonight over Marion's new job, but also a calculated grilling about Mitchell Newmann. Hopefully he would still speak with his wife in the morning.

Hopefully, *she* would still have a job in the morning.

CHAPTER 7

THERE WAS AN UNUSUAL AMOUNT of camaraderie, unanimity, and collaboration among the workers at Casebolt House. Joe Vandervelde casually spread the word that Brittany was on trial with the job, and if she failed to finish the required rooms by June first with flying colors, she would be fired and the entire crew dismissed; someone else would be given the task of finishing the remainder of the mansion. Since the restoration project promised steady employment throughout the entire summer, each man was more than eager to prove he was equal to the strain of an impossible deadline.

Brittany hated to go back to her apartment at night, there were so many little details and loose ends to tie up. Long after Joe had left, she would still be inspecting the rooms, pretending she was decorating them for her husband and child. Only perfection was good enough.

Part of each day she continued to spend in her office taking care of her other projects. After a week of rushing back and forth, she noticed her load had been considerably lightened. Donna finally confided that it was due to Lewis' intervention.

When Brittany peeked into his office to voice her thanks, Lewis admitted it was in lieu of his own appreciation of her generous hiring of Marion. He was finding his wife's enthusiasm contagious and looked forward to evenings when she would share her progress and new 'finds.' "She's like a new wife, Brittany, with all the loving traits of the old one. I'll be in your debt for months to come."

"Consider it payment for your counseling service, Lewis. Any way you look at it, I'm sure I came out ahead. Marion has more pep than a dozen workers, and fairly oozes with talent. I need her."

Not once since their date had Brit laid eyes on Doug Kennedy. Several nights in a row, she had tried to reach him at his apartment, to no avail. Finally, she left a note for him in his office suggesting a time when he might reach her. If Mitch had placed the same strict deadlines on Doug, he was no doubt working long hours, too.

Ten days into the project, Brittany was up to her elbows in activity. A steady crew of twenty worked feverishly—often in ten-hour shifts—to accomplish the goals laid out on the schedule drawn up by Joe and herself. As the work progressed, and the changes became noticeable, she grew more and more attached to the house. In her mind, she was convinced Mitch would recognize the rightness of their being together again, and the restoration became a symbol of her love for him.

Today, she determined to tackle the time-consuming and tedious task of removing all the solid brass hardware from the dozens of doors in the mansion. They were filthy and corroded beyond recognition, and she had discovered their value accidentally while trying to pick open a locked closet. Once they were repolished to their original bright sheen, the knobs would contribute handsomely to the overall worth of the house, and save Mitch several hundred dollars in replacement charges.

Three hours after beginning with the first door, Brit was still upstairs with two rooms to go. Her back ached from bending over; she was filthy from handling the tarnished hardware and spending half the time on her knees; she had broken several fingernails over stubborn screws, and she was ready to scream from plain fatigue.

The simple objective had become a major chore, and she was almost wishing she had left the job to a workman even though it would take him away from more important work. Somehow, the repetitiousness had struck a wrong chord and she was becoming edgy. Of course, part of it was probably due to the fact that Joe had left the house early on business. Every few minutes, one of the crew chiefs would interrupt her with a question needing her immediate attention; work would come to a standstill without her help. What could she say?

Brushing the tangle of raven curls off her face with growing impatience, she threw the screws from the last door into the already-full carton, followed in quick succession by the tools that had become almost attached to her hands. Flexing her fingers in delight, she leaned against a wall and allowed her shoulders to sag. She could use a few minutes respite before beginning on the downstairs rooms—if possible, in peaceful solitude.

Wrapping her arms around her head, she stretched her back muscles. Obviously, that was out of the question as long as she remained in the house. The sounds of hammering, electric saws, sanders and blaring radios filled the empty rooms, and reverberated ten-fold.

In the midst of all this chaos, Brit thought she saw a stranger step over the rubble on the first floor.

Weighted down with the heavy carton of knobs, plates and hinges, she worked her way down the sweeping stairway of the central entrance hall to investigate, feeling cautiously for each step, and trying to peer around and over the box.

"A-Alexis!" she choked, stumbling on the last stair at the same time she spotted the woman. "I didn't know you were here."

Cool, glassy-blue eyes assessed her appearance from head to foot. "I saw no reason to bother you, Miss Lawson."

Brittany placed the box on the floor and pushed it into a corner, using the activity to surreptitiously search the area for another familiar face. There were no visible signs of Mitch. Good. She hated the idea of being compared to an impeccably-dressed, beautifully-coifed woman who looked as though she had never known a moment of sweat-producing work in her life.

"If you're looking for Mr. Newmann, he isn't here right now, Alexis. I'd be happy to take a message for you."

Brit cringed inwardly. Her voice had been so thickly sugared, it made her ill. She used the pretense of brushing off a layer of dust from her hands and jeans to cover her discomfort, and prayed for help in controlling her runaway emotions.

"Yes, I'm sure you would," her visitor mused. "As Mitchell isn't due back in town until tomorrow evening, that hardly seems necessary."

Touche. The woman wasn't fooling around.

Brit hooked her thumbs through the belt loops of her pants and shrugged. "I forgot he was away. Why are you here, then? As you can see, things are pretty much in a muddle. There's debris everywhere, and I'd hate for you to ruin your clothing."

Dismissing her concern with as little attention as it deserved, Alexis left her to walk into the living room. "I'm here to inspect the mansion for Mitchell. The poor darling has been beside himself with responsibilities, and is deeply concerned over his inability to oversee the restoration. I assured him I would be happy to help you out."

Brit followed her. "I'm sorry if Mr. Newmann feels he has cause for concern, Alexis. Quite frankly, I'm rather surprised to hear that, since he hired me precisely because he knew my work first-hand, and trusted my judgment. On more than one occasion, he indicated I was to take *sole* responsibility for the project, from the initial planning to the finished, completely furnished house."

"Come now, Miss Lawson, surely you didn't take that verbatim. At the time, Mitchell probably wanted to surprise me, but now—well, you can certainly understand why I want to have a hand in deciding the color schemes and arrangements."

Alexis smiled demurely and adjusted the position of her black lizard purse under the crook of her right arm. A large square-cut diamond winked gloatingly from a ring adorning the fourth finger of her left hand.

Brittany blanched and fell silent in the moment of awkwardness. So Mitch had proposed to her after all. If Alexis wanted to alter every single plan so carefully and lovingly drawn up, it was her right as the future mistress of Casebolt House.

Swallowing convulsively, Brit nodded agreement to Alexis' comment. Where was Mitch, and why hadn't he bothered to inform her of the change in plans? The rat! Miss Marion would be heartbroken. There was no way the dear lady could continue on the project now. In fact, she couldn't continue herself.

"What did you have in mind for this room, Miss Lawson?" Alexis had finished her inspection of the living room, and had entered the adjoining library.

Brit stayed in the doorway, and watched her open and close several bookcase doors. "It was my intention to keep the room as it is, Alexis. The

104

mahogany paneling is in lovely condition. With minimal refinishing, it can be returned to its original mellow sheen; likewise, the truly beautiful parquet floor.''

"No, no, that would never do. It's much too dark and gloomy in here. We must open it up somehow, make it bright and airy. Can't we paint the paneling in some lovely pastel shade? Mauve would be nice. Yes, a subtle shade of mauve would be most unusual. The shades of lavender are a decorating rage this year.''

Alexis moved purposefully toward the window, flicked a finger over the dusty sills, and turned to survey the room once more with narrowed eyes.

"With heavy silk draperies the exact shade of the paint, and carpeting custom-dyed to match, this will make a perfect card room. Quite elegant, in fact. There is ample space for at least three table arrangements, don't you agree?" She faced Brit, immensely pleased with her moment of inspiration.

"It seems a shame to change the character of the room so drastically." Brit's stomach was in knots, and she fought for control of both her emotional involvement and her tongue. "I had thought Mit— Mr. Newmann would use this as his home office, and I know he likes . . ."

Alexis swept by her. "Obviously, you've had no experience living in the home of a socially prominent person, Miss Lawson. Mitchell and I will be expected to entertain a great deal. This mansion might have survived its Victorian beginnings intact, but its twentieth-century inhabitants needn't return it to rocking chairs and crocheted doilies. It would never do for poor Mitchell to be classified as an old-fashioned relic in his line of work.''

"Surely there's a happy meeting somewhere between the two, Alexis. I don't understand how you can feel this way when you're, apparently, such an active member of the conservation societies in San Francisco."

"One has nothing to do with the other, for goodness' sake! As a woman of some standing, I'm expected to lend my name, support, and money to many causes, but I'm not obligated to live my personal life under those rules."

"I see." Brittany studied the pattern of graining in the wood planking under her feet. It was difficult to trace through the accumulation of grime. She had looked forward to cleaning it. "It was my understanding Mr. Newmann wanted a fairly faithful restoration of this house, with only minimal changes made. I'm not a professional interior decorator, Alexis; my training is in restoration architecture, and that means I return houses to their *former* states. Perhaps you should discuss your ideas with Mitch—your fiancé—before my crews continue with their assignments. At the same time, you might want to discuss hiring someone else to take charge."

"My goodness, it's much too late for that now, Miss Lawson. You can't abandon this project for us in mid-stream. I merely suggested we collaborate on our ideas. I'm perfectly content to accompany you on a tour of the rooms and offer a recommendation or two. Surely you can't object to that. My only interest is in saving Mitchell the expense and time later, should your plans not be entirely suitable. You are an unmarried woman, after all, and can't be expected to know the needs of a family."

Brit felt the tension in the back of her neck spread upward to her temples. She stopped a cutting retort by clamping her teeth together. After counting to ten as slowly as she could, her overwhelming disappointment was under reasonable control. This was only a job like any other. Her personal feelings toward the house and its owner gave her no right to inflate it into anything else.

"Perhaps you're right, Alexis. I won't be able to take that tour with you today, however, as I have a busy schedule already. Could I get back to you in a day or two?" She moved her mouth into a ghostly semblance of a smile, but no part of it reached her eyes.

Alexis Seifert lifted her chin, the smug look of victory worn like a banner across her face. "That will be fine. I'll wait for your call."

Brittany stepped back from the doorway, and waited for her to pass by into the living room, but wasted no time finding a reason to beat a hasty exit from her presence. "Thanks for stopping by, Alexis. If you'll excuse me now, I have an appointment with my foreman." She nodded curtly and began the long walk across the empty room.

"Miss Lawson, one more thing." Alexis hurried after her, catching up inside the front hall. Her face took on a thoughtful expression while she searched for words. "I feel rather foolish having to ask this." She dug into her purse and extracted a ring of car keys, fingering them delicately with slender fingers tipped with long, painted nails, every one filed to the same length.

Brit waited, wondering about her new discovery that she actually had the ability to hate another human being. *Forgive me, Lord.* When her minister had chosen the eleventh and twelfth chapters of Romans for his sermon a few weeks earlier, she had prided herself on never falling prey to that sin. The words of the Apostle Paul came back to her. *Don't cherish exaggerated ideas of yourself or your importance, but try to have a sane estimate of your capabilities by the light of the faith that God has given to you . . . let us have no imitation Christian love . . . let us have real warm affection for one another . . . and a willingness to let the other man have the credit . . . and as for those who try to make your life a misery, bless them. Don't curse, bless . . . live at peace with everyone. Never take vengeance into your own hands. . . .*

"I must ask you to share a little secret with me, Miss Lawson," Alexis continued, peering at her closely to gauge her response. "Mitchell and I had agreed to keep our betrothal between ourselves ... until we make the announcement together. Mitchell's afraid that once the public knows, we'll be bombarded with social bookings in our honor, and he doesn't have the time right now. He'd never forgive me for my inadvertent slip this morning. I'm afraid I got carried away in my eagerness to help him with the preparations for our house. We don't want to burden him with additional problems, do we?"

Brit assumed a guarded expression. Why did she have the creeping feeling something was wrong? "I'm not sure what you're asking of me, Alexis. Mr. Newmann's personal life isn't an issue in my contract. I'm not interested in discussing his impending marriage with him." In fact, she would avoid the topic like she would a discussion of obscenities. Already, the pain from Alexis's announcement had infiltrated her heart.

'I can count on you never to mention the matter?" Alexis forced the issue one more time.

"Yes, of course. I won't say a word." Brit spoke in a rush, wanting nothing more than to get away and lick her wounds in private.

"Thank you, Miss Lawson. And, about my reason for coming here today— our collaboration on the restoration—we'll keep that to ourselves, too. I want to surprise Mitchell later with my role."

"Whatever you say, Alexis."

"Thank you, again. I'll speak with you in a couple of days about that tour of ours. You will call me?"

"Yes, yes, I'll call you." A trace of impatience crept into Brit's reply, and she saw Alexis' eyebrows rise in surprise. *Lord, I can't help it. Every time she says 'Miss Lawson' in that holier-than-thou voice of hers, I feel anger well up inside. I feel exactly like*

Paul when he said, 'my own behavior baffles me. For I find myself not doing what I really want to do but doing what I really loathe . . . I have the will to do good, but not the power.'

"Fine. Then I'll be off. I need to buy a new dress for tomorrow evening. I can never tell these days if we will be in the papers or not." She crinkled her eyes as she smiled this time, but they still mocked Brit's easy defeat.

Brit waited until she heard Alexis' car leave, and then headed directly for the kitchen in long, determined strides. She had completely lost her patience and composure. Recklessly pushing through the debris blocking her way, she ignored the curious looks of the workmen removing layers of cracked paint from cupboards, and banged out the back door.

"Going somewhere, Miss Lawson?" The master carpenter yelled at her from a temporary workshop set up in the garage.

"Home!" She didn't break stride, and totally disregarded his interest in prolonging the discussion.

"How long will you be there?" He made the inquiry as she opened her car door.

"All day!"

"Can we call you if we run into a problem?"

"No!" Slamming the car door, she neatly cut off any more communication. She didn't care what the man thought of her. Let him handle his own problems. She had enough of her own.

By the time Brittany stormed into her apartment, her emotions had taken a complete roller coaster ride. *Again.* It seemed to be a recurring problem since Mitchell Newmann's untimely appearance on the West Coast.

Flopping onto the couch, she stretched out full-length, and stared up at the ceiling. The blankness of the ceiling made a good scratch pad. For a period of time, she scribbled her thoughts across it, attempting to be rational in the process. It was a struggle, because her emotions were seldom rational these days . . . if ever. One moment she was charging forth with the confidence and determination of a Salvation Army sergeant armed with God's Word; the next, she was withdrawing into a corner, feeling as rejected, teary, and inadequate as a chastised school child.

Was it because she was a woman? Because she was still in her twenties? Because of the disappointments of life? Probably all of them had a bearing, but she had to do something about it anyway. She simply *could not* continue with the emotional seesawing of another day, not only to save wear and tear on her own frazzled nerves, but more importantly, to keep from sinning against innocent bystanders. Within the past hour, she had been rude, inconsiderate, and filled with self-pity and hate.

Rolling onto her side, Brit hugged a pillow, and closed her eyes. This was one of those times she wished her mother were close by. She would know exactly what to do. She was one of the finest Christian women she had ever known, with a faith so strong a bull-dozer couldn't budge it. A conversation with her over the telephone might perk up her spirits, but it would be impossible to explain exactly how she felt, especially since she had never mentioned Mitch to her parents. They still had no idea he was the reason she had fled to California after graduation.

Tears rolled from the corners of her eyes, but she let them continue unchecked. She was entitled to a moment of self-pity. It certainly wasn't unusual for a woman to cry over a man once in awhile. There was no reason to add guilt over that to all of her other problems. If there was one thing she felt confident about at this moment, it was the certainty of God's understanding of her feelings, of His willingness to forgive her for falling from grace yet another morning, and of His patience with her fumbling attempts to put

110

her relationship with Mitch in the proper perspective in her life. God knew what was in her heart and mind already. He would stand by while she licked her wounds, and then provide the right dose of medicine to get her up on her feet again. He always did.

In the middle of her ponderings, the doorbell startled her with jarring abruptness. Her eyes flew open, but otherwise, she stayed rigid on the couch. No one she knew would expect to find her home in the middle of the day. There was no need to answer.

The bell pealed again, longer this time.

Brit felt the hard, dull thumps of her heart, and unconsciously began counting the rings with her eyes riveted on the door. She had forgotten to relock it. The chain hung loose.

The bell continued without let-up.

Suddenly, an angry knocking shook the door, and had her leaping to her feet. Who was the maniac? Maybe she should call the manager.

"Open up, Brit! I know you're in there."

It was Mitch! She couldn't face him now. She didn't want to ever see him again. How could she? What could she say? Throwing the tightly-clutched pillow onto the couch, Brittany took a hasty swipe at her eyes and started for the door at the same time it was flung open.

Equally surprised, both Mitch and Brittany stood motionless, as though held under the power of a hypnotic spell. Mitch was the first to recover. He pushed the door closed with one hand while continuing to examine her in minute detail. His troubled eyes left her only long enough to make one quick search of the room. By the time they returned to her face, he had located the purse where she had thrown it upon entering the apartment, had observed the crushed hollow shape on the couch, and the dark circle where her tears had fallen. He was ready with questions.

"What happened?" His voice was soft with gentle

concern, and Brit ached to throw herself into his arms and tell him.

"I thought you were out of town, and not due back until t-tomorrow," she hedged, clearing the huskiness from her throat.

"I got back early. Why did you leave the site?"

"I—I wanted a day off, Mitch. I've been working hard for days now." Her eyes fell before his steady scrutiny.

"Just like that? The men said you rushed away like the place was on fire. What happened, Brit? Did you have an accident?"

"No, it was nothing, Mitch. Really." Her throat tightened severely while she attempted to keep her lower jaw from trembling. Why was he being so solicitous, and . . . and kind? Why was he so heart-breakingly handsome in his white dress shirt?

"Don't you feel well?"

"I feel . . . f-fine." At least she felt better now, knowing he seemed to care.

"You don't look it." His voice came petal-soft at the same time his hand came up to cup her chin, and lift her face for his perusal. "You've been crying."

"I have not."

"Yes, you have, Brit." His faint smile warmed her heart, and she began to tremble; he was promised to another woman. "You have dirt smudges and streaks of mascara all over your face."

"All right, I was c-crying!" She pushed his hand away, and quipped, "I'm *entitled* to cry whenever I want!"

The sharpness of her retort worked like a pitcher of water on Mitch's compassion. The cold winter steel in his eyes matched the ice in his next question. "Not on my time, you're not. Did one of the workmen say something? Did one of them dare to lay his hands on you?" He stepped forward to grip her arms and his touch sparked immediate gooseflesh.

"No!" Her dark eyes flew to meet his narrowly-veiled inspection. Her breath was practically stolen from her body at the sight of his fury, and her entire being responded to his disquietude and the chaotic disturbance of his nearness. "But if one of them *had*, it's my business, Mitch! It has *nothing* to do with you!"

Taking deep breaths through flared nostrils, Mitch struggled for control of his temper. A nervous twitching played at the corners of his finely-chiseled jaw, and his mouth thinned to a straight line. "Your diversionary tactics won't work this time, Brittany. I demand to know what happened at the site to send you home in the middle of the day!"

An answering leap of fire brought a flush of red to Brit's cheeks. "You have no right to make demands of me and I don't intend to tell you." She had intended to be equally icy, but the dryness of her throat softened the protest to an aching whisper. Why had she made her stupid promise to Alexis? It would serve her right if she broke it and got her deliberately in trouble with Mitch. All was fair in love or war, wasn't it?

"We'll see about that." Not once had Mitch taken his eyes off her face, and something he saw there must have touched a nerve. With a sharp intake of air, he pulled her closer. "Maybe I should shake some sense into you."

"I don't respond to roughness, or tough talk, or threats, or demands of any kind, Mr. Newmann. It only succeeds in making me mad, so let me go!" She made an attempt to free herself from his talon-like hold.

"I'll let you go as soon as you tell me why you're home crying. I'm not trying to punish you, Brit; I'm trying to help!" He shook her gently a couple of times, raising his own voice in the process.

"This kind of help I don't need!" she spouted back,

113

grasping the upper sleeves of his shirt to steady herself. His muscles rippled under her fingers, and she caught her lip under her front teeth to bite back the gasp of pleasure that being near him gave her.

Abruptly, Mitch's struggles with her ceased. As he gazed into her luminous black eyes, the harsh lines on his face softened. His hands slipped from her arms, and moved to wrap around her narrow waist. For several seconds, he seemed to drink in the sight of her before his lips twisted into a crooked smile. "You gypsy," he drawled, using one hand to push away the tumble of raven curls that had fallen across her face. "You've got my blood singing again."

His lips drifted downward, and there was plenty of time to protest. Another time, she might have the will to resist, but not this one, not today. This kiss might be her last from him. His lips grazed hers in soft feathery strokes, eliciting a muffled sound from her throat. "Mitch . . . Mitch," she whispered, her lips moving under the pressure of his.

He stopped to rest his forehead against hers. He sighed heavily, and the heat of his aspiration fanned her face. *Kiss me, Mitch, kiss me properly.* She wanted to beg him, and alternately, to initiate it herself. But she waited in the agony of insecurity, lest she end the moment of closeness.

His arm tightened around her waist, pushing the last breath of air from her lungs, and again, she held back her protest and waited.

Slowly she felt his face shift against hers, and her lips opened in readiness, like a rosebud to the morning dew. At long last, they were completely covered by the velvety warmth of his. Sliding her hands around Mitch's waist, Brittany clung to his body. Did he share any of her deep feelings? He was still attracted to her, or he wouldn't be kissing her, but was the singing in his blood only due to that, and not a smoldering of their lost, heartfelt love?

Mitch's lips lingered against hers, gently caressing them, as though hating to let go.

"It might sound crazy to you, under the circumstances, Brit," he confessed hoarsely, his mouth moving to capture the hollow over one closed eye, "but I missed you this week."

Trembling from the joy those few words gave her, Brit kissed the tip of his chin and echoed his words in a husky whisper of her own. "I missed you too, Mitch." Her head was swimming with confusion, and unwanted thoughts kept pushing to the forefront, but she willed them to silence. She was too happy, and wanted to feel optimistic. She pressed her cheek against his. "Where did you go?" she whispered, her need to know suddenly important.

Mitch was silent for some time, grazing his lips restlessly across her forehead. "I had to fly to Denver."

"Why didn't you call me before you went?"

"There wasn't time."

Unconsciously, Brit's back stiffened. "That's a little hard to believe."

Mitch's embrace weakened, and although he still held her, she felt a widening chasm between them. "Why is that?"

"No reason. It was a dumb thing to say." She tightened her arms around him, and pressed her cheek against his chest, enjoying the hard drumming of his heart. Why had she ruined her last precious moment in his embrace? Was the Lord using her jealousy to work against herself this time? She had no right to be in Mitch's arms.

"I don't think so." He held her from him, and studied her intently. "What did you mean, Brit?"

"You seemed to have enough time to call your fian—" Just in time, she caught herself, and avoided meeting his troubled gaze while finishing rather meekly "—your Alexis."

115

"How do you know that?" His brows met together over the bridge of his perfect nose.

"How do you think I know! *She* told me!"

"It isn't necessary to raise your voice, Brit. Did you call Alexis, looking for me?" He was clearly puzzled.

"Can't we drop the subject, Mitch?"

"Can't you give me a simple yes or no?"

"If it's so important for you to know, then *no*, I did *not* call her!"

"Then how *did* you learn she knew where I was?"

"I already answered that. She told me."

" *When?* " Mitch's lips compressed tightly.

Brit lifted her hands and dropped them again in a gesture of futility. "Today!" she snapped.

"Where?"

"At the house! Now are you pleased with yourself?" She pulled herself free with a rough jerk, sending him a look of venom.

Mitch's eyebrows went up at her outburst, but he didn't immediately reply. From her perch on the arm of the couch, Brit watched him warily. He was too intelligent to miss putting two and two together. She had already said too much; he had a way of getting under her thin skin.

During interminable seconds, Mitch stroked his jaw with restless fingers. His eyes were veiled from her by half-closed lids while he pretended to study the covers of *Architectural Digest* magazines lying on the coffee table between them.

"Do you have any cold sodas in the house?"

His question was unexpected. "I—I think so."

"Stay there. I'll get it." He stopped her movement with a hand on her arm. "Would you like one?"

"No, thanks." Brit stared after him, frowning. He intended to stay a while longer. She would need to be doubly cautious now, or he would soon have her babbling like an idiot over her altercation with Alexis.

116

Seeking the support of something solid under her, she curled up in one corner of the couch and draped her arm over the edge, resting her head against 'it. Winning the love and respect of a man—the right man—was not in any way, shape, or form a simple task.

Closing her eyes in weariness, Brittany tried to remember all Mitch's good points—the ones which had caused her to fall in love with him. There were too many to enumerate. She had first been attracted by his eyes—the way they sparkled with interest in eveyone and everything around him. Then she had learned of his generosity to people who worked for him. Word had gotten around the site of his incredibly caring ways. He had provided all the money for a liver transplant when a construction worker's young son was at the brink of death, and put his private jet at their disposal for flying the entire family to the city where the donor had expired in an accident.

After that, she had found herself filling the pages of her diary with accounts of his ceaseless work with various charities. It seemed they all wanted a portion of whatever he was willing to give, and he always gave something, without fanfare. More often than not, it was a gift of his time, love and talent, not his money. One evening she had gone with him to a pancake supper, given by a Baltimore church to raise money for a nursing home. Mitch wasn't even a member of the church. He had heard about it from one of the electricians at Harborplace, and volunteered to help serve the pancakes.

She admired that trait of unselfishness. But now, it was off set by the glaring error causing their estrangement. Why hadn't he told her about his former wife and his daughter? She had never given him an opportunity to explain. Would he, if she were to ask him now?

A stirring in the room caused her eyelids to flutter

open. Mitch was sitting in the club chair across from the couch. "You look like a young teenager in those rolled-up jeans and bare feet, Brit. I'm having trouble remembering you're an experienced architect and fellow professional." The warmth of his smile and the friendliness of his tone of voice threatened to tear her apart at the seams. She would not break down in front of him.

"I—I probably shouldn't wear them anymore. I'm getting too old," she said jerkily.

"You have the figure for them, and there aren't any age limits for wearing jeans these days." He took a swig of grape soda from a perspiring can and watched her with lazy eyes. Heightened awareness still quivered in the space between them. "You look a little tired today. Maybe it's a good thing you came home after all," he said quietly. "Was there some special reason you needed to get in touch with me this week? Are there problems at Casebolt House?"

"No, not really. Everything is on schedule . . . so far." She paused and examined the broken nails on one still very dirty hand. "Mitch . . ." she began hesitantly, weighing her words with greater care. "I need to clarify a few things with you."

"About the house?"

Brittany looked up and his steady eyes met hers. "Yes," she said, her normally husky voice deepened by the breathlessness his look evoked, "about . . . the house."

"All right. I'm listening."

"I need to know whether or not you've changed your mind about anything."

"About the house?"

"Mitch, please," she protested, but in the end, met his teasing grin with one of her own.

"You'll have to be more specific, Brittany. Changed my mind about what?" He was serious now, one professional to another, and it was easier for her to continue.

118

"When you commissioned me to do the restoration on Casebolt House, you said you trusted my judgment entirely. You gave me free reign to do with it as I saw fit. I remember telling you I thought it should be quite faithfully *restored*, not remodeled or modernized, except for a few necessary changes to meet today's living standards." She paused, and immediately felt her heart hammering in double-time against her ribs. Somehow she had to discover how much support he would provide against Alexis' disastrous plans.

"I remember all of our discussions, Brittany. Is there some problem about the restoration? Can't it be done?" He was studying her closely, his dove-gray eyes alert and penetrating.

"Oh, yes, it can be done, and . . . and there's no problem about doing it that way. I—I was just wondering if . . . whether or not you had changed your mind since then . . . for some reason." Now it would come. Her head was throbbing from the tension.

"No, I haven't."

"Not at all?" He apparently wasn't thinking straight. Once Alexis and he had an opportunity to be together again, he would hear of her plans and understand her interest in having a hand in decorating her future home. "You don't want your . . . the people who are to live there . . . to have a hand in the planning?"

"That isn't possible right now, unfortunately."

"But what about . . ." Something warned her to be quiet, and she swallowed Alexis' name.

"I spoke with Hally about your plans for her room, and she seemed to like everything I mentioned. Her one request was for a 'super-sized' bed to facilitate overnight guests." Mitch placed the empty soda can on the table and leaned forward with his elbows on his knees. While deeply engraved lines ridged his forehead, he played with the band of his watch. Suddenly, he peered up at Brit. "I want to explain why I was unable to reach you before leaving town."

She attempted to stop him, but his seriousness prohibited an interruption. There was a hint of some rare emotion she didn't recognize in his eyes.

"I was attending a dinner given in my honor a couple days after being with you . . ." His voice trailed to a stop.

Brittany lowered her lashes. She remembered that meeting in detail.

"The hotel operator called with an urgent message from Hally. My mother suffered another severe attack of angina, and had been taken to the hospital."

"I'm so sorry, Mitch. Is she all right now?"

"Yes, she's home again for the time being. I intended to call you several times, Brittany, but there were lists of matters needing my attention, and somehow I was never in the right place at the right time."

"I understand."

"I hope you do. I didn't call Alexis either, by the way. She was attending the dinner party, and volunteered to drive me to the airport."

"I see." Brit's mouth curved into a smile. "Mitch, one of the reasons I was trying to reach you concerns your mother. Will she sell her home in Denver, and live with you in Casebolt House?"

"Yes. Her ill health is the primary reason for getting it ready with some degree of urgency. I should have discussed it with you before, but as you know by now, I'm a comparatively private person."

"That, sir, is an understatement, I believe." Brittany had difficulty meeting his eyes once again, and drew a shaky breath. She had finally regained his confidence. It was a step in the right direction. "Mitch, will your mother be bringing much of her furniture and personal belongings? It would simplify decorating decisions considerably if I knew what pieces were available."

"I discussed that with her on one of the hospital visits. We decided it would be best to take as little as possible. I have a list of the few things that carry the most sentimental value. They are being shipped. The remainder of the household will be turned over to an auction house."

Mitch spoke matter-of-factly, but Brit knew there was a deeper level of sensitivity locked inside him. She had been given a brief glimpse of his vulnerability when he confessed he had missed her this week. He needed an open ear, a caring soul to use as a sounding board. He had Alexis, but with all her intuition about people, Britanny knew his choice for a new wife could never bring him the support he sought in times of great need or comforting.

"It must be heart-breaking for your mother to leave her home after living there so many years. I'll do everything I can to have things ready for all of you. I've asked Marion Stanford to be the interior decorator, by the way. She's ecstatic over the challenge, and has made great strides this week. She knows the history of this city by heart, has an enormous respect for it, and yet she is as up-to-date and modern in her thinking as any younger decorator I know."

She stopped to assess his reaction and added, "I hope you approve, Mitch. She'd be crushed if I had to dismiss her for any reason."

"I approve, heartily. Between the two of you, you'll manage to do everything right. I'll call and tell her myself."

"Then, you *want* me to continue with the restoration *exactly* as we had discussed, with *no* drastic changes? And you *want* Miss Marion to stay on as the decorator, in *sole charge* of turning Casebolt House into a home for you and your family?"

"Yes, I do, Brittany."

When Brittany breathed an audible sigh of relief, Mitch shook his head slowly. "It would have saved us considerable time if you had come out with it when I first walked into your apartment, you know."

Brittany's eyes widened. "Come out with what?"

Mitch laughed and rose from the chair, holding out a hand to pull her from the couch. "I will not participate in another of your try-to-bluff-him games, so forget the innocence act. It took a while, but I've been able to elicit through our conversation that Alexis visited Casebolt House today, and in her own inimitable way, managed to persuade you *she* could do a better job, and if you would only follow her advice, everything would be perfect. She has a remarkable talent for organization and enjoys taking charge." He pressed her hands together between his and noticed the broken nails and layers of black grime. "What I don't understand, Gypsy, is why you let her, and why it upset you to the point of rushing home to cry."

Stung by the idea that he had confided his concerns merely to throw her off balance and get her talking about her crying jag, Brit steeled herself against his dominating presence, and her powerful yearning to answer his questions truthfully. Was it any less honorable to break a promise to someone than to lie to another in order to keep it?

"You are entitled to your own interpretation, Mitch, but I'll neither confirm nor deny its validity. Why I was crying is a personal matter, and I don't intend to discuss it with you." She withdrew her hands from his and jammed them into her jeans pockets. "However, the matter of Casebolt House does need discussing." She walked over to pick up her purse from the floor, placing it onto the coffee table.

"You know yourself it's highly unusual for an architect to have complete charge of a project, Mitch, especially if it's a restoration. We need input and approval from the owners of the property. To tell you the truth, I'm becoming rather jittery about the responsibility you've foisted on me.''

"You needn't be."

"I'm grateful you feel that way, but I've been thinking it might be better for Marion and me to have something more than your oral assurances.'' To cover her trembling fingers, Brittany picked up the empty soda can next to her purse, and twirled it around in her hands. Mitch watched her in a contemplative mood, his arms crossed in front of his chest.

"Such as?''

Brit shrugged and headed toward the kitchen. "Such as either daily consultations or a statement in writing.'' She flung the suggestion over her shoulder as she left the room.

He followed her. "I don't have time for daily consultations, Brittany. That's why I hired you—to eliminate having them.''

"Then a written statement will have to do. It's for your protection as well as ours, Mitch.'' She threw the can into the garbage and turned on the faucet at the sink to wash her hands.

"I've never had my word questioned before, but if a written statement will make you feel safer, then I'll gladly provide one. What should it say?'' He perched on a stool, and rolled the cuffs of his dress shirt up to his elbows.

"I'd like it to state, in no uncertain terms, that you have granted Marion Stanford and myself freedom to restore and decorate Casebolt House as we see fit, that our decisions and choices are not to be changed without a direct order from you, in person or in writing.''

Mitch observed her with some amusement. "You're serious about this.''

"Yes, I most certainly am.''

"Exactly who will be shown this document?'' He rubbed the side of his nose and stroked an eyebrow,

123

tilting his head to peer at her from the corners of his eyes. It was a provocative pose, and she braced herself against the sink. She felt as weak and limp as a rag doll. Mitch was irresistible when he chose to be charming.

"Workmen. Or *whoever* gets a notion to interfere, or work at cross purpose with our decisions." The dimples trembled in her cheeks.

"I see." He hadn't been able to trick her into using Alexis' name. "I can't imagine anyone having the temerity to question your decisions, but if you need a paper, I'll provide one."

"Thank you."

His crooked grin made him disturbingly attractive, and Brit drew in her breath sharply. She had achieved her objectives. Mitch had granted her his unqualified support, and Casebolt House would be protected against ruthless destruction by an uncaring dilettante.

"Happy now?" Mitch asked.

"Yes."

"There won't be any more tears?" He was deliberately baiting her again.

"There will be if you leave here without presenting me with that document. Come right this way, if you please, sir. I happen to have a pen and paper waiting in my workroom." She motioned for him to follow her.

Seated at her desk, he paused before beginning to write. "Why don't you get cleaned up, Miss Lawson, and we'll both play hookey the rest of the day. You can show me around Fisherman's Wharf and Pier 39. I'd like to check out my competition to see what I'm up against. I can't have my redevelopment project come up second- or third-best."

His casual invitation caught her unaware, but once she had reined her galloping pulse, she found it comparatively easy to match his off-handedness. "All right, I might as well go along. I'm not going to throw

124

away the opportunity to discuss your house while I can. Give me a few minutes to take a shower.''

"See that you don't dawdle. There's no need to doll up. We won't go anywhere fancy.''

"I'll take as long as I need, and wear what I choose!'' The sound of his laughter was like music to her ears.

CHAPTER 8

TWO WEEKS LATER, Brittany sat slumped on the floor of Hally's bedroom at Casebolt House, reliving every minute of that half-day holiday for the hundredth time. The afternoon had stretched on into the evening hours, and Mitch had been in no hurry to end the day.

They had taken a leisurely drive of the entire Bay area—that in truth consisted of eight bays joined together by a maze of channels, islands and bridges. They discussed in depth the pros and cons of each new or restored project along the way. Mitch had shown her the area designated for his redevelopment and shared a few of his plans.

They had parked his car near Ghirardelli Square and walked every inch of the area from there, past the Cannery, Fisherman's Wharf, and on over to Pier 39 and back again—the entire northeast waterfront. Together, the four developments formed a monumental montage of restaurants, shops, cabarets, and amusements cleverly designed to enhance the picturesque bay where hundreds of fishing boats berthed daily. Through ingenious restoration of a former chocolate factory and fruit cannery, the once defunct area had become a famous and popular thoroughfare for the aimless, local pedestrians, and tourists alike.

She and Mitch had slipped into their old affinity with unbelievable ease. Their eyes had witnessed and appreciated the beauty around them, their equally quick minds had raced to similar conclusions on myriad subjects, and their conversation had been both stimulating and satisfying. They had laughed and joked, teased and argued, and not once broken the enjoyment of the experience with a reference to their past or present relationships.

At least, not until she had gotten carried away after being entertained by a roller-skating accordionist-clown, and turned impulsively to Mitch. "I can't wait to see what Hally thinks of all this! Won't she love the cable cars and all these fascinating, eccentric street people?"

"Yes," he had nodded, strangely quiet, "I suspect she will."

Fortunately a crowd of boisterous tourists had edged them off the sidewalk, and the distraction had given them an opportunity to laugh and a more neutral topic of discussion.

Mitch had suggested they have dinner together when the car came into view at the end of their stroll, and, eager to prolong her time with him, she had agreed. "Sure, why not? I'm not against eliminating an evening of dish washing when the chance is presented to me." Her quick repartee had made him chuckle, and he had taken her hand and led her into Maxwell's Plum, a luxurious restaurant in Ghirardelli Square, which had an unobstructed view of a beautiful expanse of The Bay, Alcatraz Island, and the City, through two-storied walls of glass. Dim candlelight, fresh spring roses, soft music, and linens in various shades of pink created a magical aura of quiet intimacy.

There had been long lulls in their conversation during a delicious seafood dinner, but they hadn't been uncomfortable ones. With highly imaginative thoughts of romance, she had been able to feast unobtrusively on Mitch's unutterably handsome face while he watched the progress of sloops with billowing spinnakers race seaward across the bay.

On the way back to her apartment, neither of them had broken the silence in the dark interior of his car. Block after city block, she had wondered whether he would ask to come in for coffee, and the anticipation of the familiarity it might precipitate brought the greatest happiness she had felt for years.

He hadn't. He had pulled up next to the curb fronting her apartment, and turned without a trace of anything but friendly politeness on his face. "I won't walk you in tonight, Brittany. I still have a couple things to do before turning in. Thanks for your time tonight. I enjoyed it."

"Sure," she had mumbled. "Anytime. Glad I could be of some help. Thanks for the dinner."

"I owed you one," he had said, raising his hand to gently squeeze her shoulder before leaning across her body to open the car door.

She had frozen against the plush seat until he was no longer brushing against her with his arm. "When will I see you again, Mitch?" It had sounded like a straightforward question, but it had been loaded with unspoken innuendo. How she had prayed he would understand it had nothing to do with business between them!

"I can't say for sure, Brit. I'll be pretty busy over the next several days. Try leaving any messages you might have with the hotel operator, or with one of the secretaries at the Forty-Niners' office. I'll be in and out of there, between trying to set up office space for my team of designers and meeting with them on the development situation."

"Well, you know where to look if you need me for anything," she had responded cheerfully.

Too cheerfully, perhaps. In spite of two calls to his hotel and office, she had neither seen nor heard from Mitch since that night, and she was miserable.

"Brittany Lawson, whatever are you doing down there?"

Brit grimaced at the sound of Marion Stanford's voice behind her, and turned her head to grin self-consciously. "Hi, Marion, I'm testing the softness of the rug you chose for Hally's room. It's perfect!"

"I must say, you think of everything. I've assailed Lewis with tales of your thoroughness, and this new one is bound to impress him. Perhaps we should push for a raise for you."

"Before you mention it, Miss Marion, I should confess I was really pretending to be young, and eyeing your work from the viewpoint of a young girl. Lewis might think I've lost my mind." Brit sprang to her feet and became more serious. "It's turning out well, isn't it? I can't wait to see it decorated with the furnishings you bought."

"It's like giving birth to a child, isn't it, dear? I had forgotten the euphoria that follows the completion of each phase of a project such as this one."

"I've never experienced childbirth, but I've seen enough movies of the process to know the labor involved is exhausting, tedious, and painful, but the end result so rewarding that the hard work is soon forgotten. We've been working hard this month, haven't we? How are you holding up, Miss Marion?"

"I have energy to burn, Brittany. I've never felt better in my life. Did I tell you your nice employer stopped by the house one evening last week?"

"No, you didn't." Brit tried to act indifferent to the sudden insertion of Mitch's name into their conversation, but could feel the rising heat in her cheeks.

"He's such a dear, sweet man, and terribly attrac-

129

tive, don't you agree?'' Marion's eyes shone like dusky diamonds. "He made a special trip to tender his personal acceptance of my appointment as the interior decorator of Casebolt House. Now, tell me that wasn't a lovely thing to do!"

"I can't, because it was. He told me he planned to call you, but I didn't think he would remember." Brit was conscious of Marion's scrutiny, and turned away to look out the window. "Was he on his way home from work?"

"I believe he did say he was returning from a work conference, of sorts. He had Mrs. Seifert with him. She heads the Save San Francisco Bay Association this year. Have you worked with her, dear?"

"No, I haven't, only with other members of the group. I've met Alexis, though. She's quite . . . stunning."

"You've met her? When was that?" Marion brushed the rug free of Brittany's imprint with her foot.

"The first time was the night after your dinner. Doug and I ran into them at the Venetian Room while celebrating his new commission."

"By 'them' you mean Mrs. Seifert and your Mitchell?"

"Who else? According to the society columns, they've become quite an item. It seems they're inseparable. Did you see their picture in the paper?" Brit's voice was sarcastic and bitter, but she couldn't help herself. It was impossible to pretend she didn't care that Mitch had never returned her calls when he seemed to have time to socialize in the evenings.

"Yes. Lewis pointed it out to me. It was a gorgeous likeness of Mitchell. I'm so glad for his sake. But, poor Alexis has never been photogenic. She hasn't aged gracefully, and tries to cover the signs with too much make-up. The rules for wearing make-up are quite simple. The older you become, the more natural

130

it should make you look. Leave the exotic colors for the young or the beautiful." Marion made a prim face at Brittany, and succeeded in making her smile. "Good, you're beginning to see the humor in the situation. For one minute, I thought you actually believed the rumors created by over-zealous gossip mongers."

"In this case, the rumors are true, Miss Marion. They're already engaged." Too late, she clamped her fingers over her mouth. Well, she hadn't promised Alexis anything more than to keep from spilling her knowledge to Mitch.

"Engaged! I can't believe it. Did Mitchell tell you that?"

"No, but Alexis did when she stopped by here to oversee the restoration one day. She was wearing a sinfully large ring, and flaunted it with great delight. She doesn't like what we're doing with her future home."

"Excuse me for being blunt, dear, but Alexis has a bad habit of showing up in places without an invitation. If it suited her purpose to make you think she was engaged to your Mitchell, I have no doubts she would manufacture a convincing story. Was the stone on her ring a five-carat square-cut diamond?"

"Yes, it was. How did you know that?"

"I thought so. If my memory serves me well, it was a gift from her first husband. Once she had met you, she apparently brought it out of storage—for your benefit. You're younger and more beautiful, and you share Mitchell's professional interests."

"*First* husband! How many have there been? What are you saying, Miss Marion?" Brittany moved from the window and took several steps toward her friend. "Are you saying Alexis might have lied to me?"

"I wasn't present during your conversation, dear, but personally, I'd be wary of an engagement that isn't made public knowledge." Marion paused and

pursed her lips, hugging her elfin body with her arms.
"Are you ready for a heart-to-heart session with me
about your Mitchell Newmann, Brittany?"

Her smile was warm and inviting, her clear blue
eyes filled with motherly empathy and understanding.
"Lewis and I are saddened by your increasing
unhappiness this month. We're not blind to what goes
on around us, even though we are in another generation. I'd like to help you if I can. I hate like the
dickens to see you with your chin dragging when this
dream project of yours means so much to you."

"I don't want to burden you with my problems,
Marion. You've done so much already." Brit felt a
familiar lump rise in her throat. It seemed to be almost
a permanent fixture these days.

Marion held out her hands. "Nothing you could
ever share with me will be a burden, child. I've got
the good Lord to lift and bear every load that becomes
too much for me to handle, and who knows, he might
just give me the right words to lighten yours, too.
Whatever you say will go no further than this room."

"You've been miscast as my interior decorator."
Brittany clasped her friend's hands, and managed a
crooked smile. "I've got a bad case of Spurned Love,
Marion, and it's almost to the terminal stage. Have
you got a cure for that, or a love potion guaranteed to
catch a man who doesn't want you?"

"I can't imagine a still-breathing man who wouldn't
want you, if given half a chance, my dear. Has
Mitchell said he doesn't?" Marion looked mildly
shocked.

Brittany felt herself blushing, and lowered her eyes.
It was difficult speaking boldly to such a gentle and
refined woman. "Well, no, sometimes he acts like he
does."

"I thought so. I knew your Mitch wasn't completely blind. Let's both test Hally's lovely blue
carpet, Brittany. We might as well be comfortable

while we make our plans." Marion hiked the level of her skirt above her knees, and squatted Indian-style on the rug, motioning for Brit to join her.

Brittany pulled her knees up under her chin. "If your husband were to drop by right now and see you in this position, I'd have a lot of explaining to do, Miss Marion."

"Nonsense. It's none of his business. Now, let's get back to Mitchell." Marion's calm blue gaze made the situation seem entirely normal. "Were you very close out in Baltimore before coming to us? Did you love each other?"

"Yes we did."

"Can you deny that Mitchell is always on your mind?"

Brittany shook her head. "He has been for five years." She broke into a wide grin, meeting her friend's twinkling eyes. Then tilting her head with a shake of incredulity, she sighed, "You're too much. You know that, don't you?"

Marion laughed heartily, her hands pressed against her cheeks. "It must come with old age."

"You'll never be old."

"You have a knack for diplomacy, dear. Now, where were we? Oh, yes—the urge to enact what has been a never-forgotten dream. Do you think Mitchell still loves you?"

"I think he might."

"You think all that old magic might still be there?"

"Yes, and even more so, perhaps." Brit hunched over, dropping her gaze to the rug. As she had an infinite number of times already, she relived the times Mitch and she had shared since that first day in Casebolt House.

"I'm not surprised. You've both stood the test of time. Your love for Mitch has grown, so your only problem is learning whether Mitch's has too, and more importantly, knowing if your lifestyles and beliefs are compatible. We've all made mistakes because we're only human beings, and in great need of God's continued guidance, love, and forgiveness. We get it, too, in abundance. Do you think you can tell me why you and Mitch separated in the first place, dear?"

Brittany shifted uncomfortably and played with the nap on the wool carpet. "You already know that Mitch was in charge of that redevelopment project in Baltimore, and that I had been assigned to fulfill my architectural internship with him. We were attracted to each other immediately. I was frightened to the point of paralysis whenever we were alone. He was several years older—a mature, famous, wealthy architect-businessman, and unbelievably handsome. He slowly gained my confidence, and then courted me patiently. We became wonderful friends—friends that fell in love. He asked me to marry him as soon as I finished my degree."

"On this special project, Mitch had been working away from home, but the week after my graduation, we went to his apartment. We planned to have that quiet time together, away from everything for the day, to set a wedding date and plan the details. While we were there, the telephone rang. There was an emergency at the site. Mitch left, and I stayed there to wait for him. Passing his bedroom to get myself a drink of water from the kitchen, I inadvertently spotted two shocking pictures. One was of his wife, and the other of his young daughter. He had never told me about them. He had never mentioned being married."

Marion nodded her understanding. "You naturally concluded he was a married man . . . a *family man* . . . who was working away from home. . . and was lonely."

Brittany nodded again. "And so I ran—all the way to San Francisco. I've tried to forget him, Marion, but . . ." She shrugged, her loss of words an eloquent statement of how much she was hurting.

"You love him. A deep, *abiding* love is an important factor in a successful relationship, Brittany, but the most significant of all, to people like you and me, is a mutual sharing of faith in God, because *then* all the other factors fall into place, and take on the right perspective. Both of you need to seek God's will in your lives, but remember He expects you to do your share of the work."

Marion stretched her legs and clicked the toes of her shoes together. "As I see it, your tragically broken romance is based on a lack of communication. When did you discover Mitchell was a widower?"

"In your home, the day he hired me."

Marion was startled by the answer, and covered Brit's hand. "What did he say when he learned of your lamentable misunderstanding?" she asked tenderly.

Tears welled up in Brit's eyes. "He doesn't know yet, at least not all of it. He thinks I left him after discovering he had a daughter."

"Oh, my, what a shame." Marion sighed and shifted positions on the rug, and chose her next words carefully. "So, after five years of bewilderment over your mysterious disappearance, Mitchell finds you, learns you know about his daughter, and for the *second* time, he's deeply hurt. The woman he wanted to marry apparently abandoned him because of an innocent, motherless child. You must tell him the truth, Brittany."

"I've tried! He won't listen to me! I haven't seen him for two weeks, and he hasn't answered either of my calls. I see those pictures of him and Alexis in the papers, and get so frustrated by the innuendoes. The very thought of him sharing *my* dream house with *that* woman kills me a little more each day I spend here!" In the passion of anger, Brit beat the floor with her fists.

"You mustn't be defeated so easily, my dear. Rest

assured Mitch isn't going to rush into marriage with Alexis, or anyone else. Not after finding you again. He needs time to sort out his feelings. In the meantime, *you* need to find more opportunities to fan the embers of your old relationship to life, that's all. You must create flames, dear . . . leaping blue flames! In the proper manner, of course," she hastened to add. "Pray about it."

Marion pulled her legs to one side and attempted to move. "Now what do I do? It was quite comfortable down here on the rug, but my body doesn't want to cooperate now that it's time to rise. You'll have to help me, Brittany."

Lifting the tiny, energetic woman to her feet, Brittany chuckled. "You weigh less than a toothpick, Miss Marion. How do you have the stamina to keep going the way you do?"

"Lewis says it's from sheer stubbornness, and he's probably right. I love the life God has given me, and while I'm here to enjoy it, I refuse to waste a minute more than necessary from the seat of a rocking chair. There is so much more to do, to experience, to learn—so much to share with those less fortunate."

"I love you, Miss Marion." Brittany hugged her impulsively. "Thank you for your encouragement and understanding."

"Pshaw, I've done nothing yet, but I intend to— tactfully and subtly, of course. It never pays to be too pushy. Now, my advice to you is this. When you get together with your Mitchell, inform him of your mistake. If he won't listen to reason, stoke the embers of his attraction to you. You know, a little kiss, a smile there," Marion said with a mischievous grin.

"I'd like to follow your advice, if I ever get the opportunity again, Marion. I've hurt Mitch deeply, and I just don't know if he thinks he can ever trust me again. I need a major miracle, I'm afraid. Mrs. Newmann and Hally arrive in a week."

"That's good. They'll be a help to you. Mitch's mother will instantly recognize you as the right woman to take over responsibility for her precious granddaughter, and what better way to prove yourself to Mitchell than to become his child's dearest friend and ally?"

Draping her arm around Marion's thin shoulders, Brittany walked her to the door of the almost-finished bedroom, and on down the hallway. "When you do decide to retire to that rocking chair, you should become a marriage broker!"

"I shall give it my uppermost consideration . . . when the time comes."

For the next few minutes, Brittany and Marion went over the shipment of furniture that had arrived from Denver, and admired how well it was being incorporated into the new household. By mutual consent, they set the date for delivery of the new pieces—which Marion had ordered and had waiting in half a dozen shops—for the next day. They walked through the rooms that Joe Vandervelde had carefully supervised, and complimented the workmen on their speed and diligence.

Joe called her aside and shifted his feet a few times before moving the ever-present cigar stub to the side of his mouth. "I was wondering if you had a chance to talk to your boss, Miss Lawson. It's my kid's birthday on Friday, and it sure would be a kick to give him that autograph. I thought I'd try to pick up a poster of the Forty-Niners for his room."

"I forgot to tell you I spoke with Mr. Newmann two weeks ago, Joe. He was pleased with the request, and said he'd pick up a few things from the office and drop them by here. He won't forget."

"How about that! He's some guy, huh?"

Brittany silently agreed before rejoining Marion, walking her out to the waiting Mercedes and Soo Ling, her patient chauffeur.

"Have you seen Douglas lately, Brittany? How is he enjoying his work on Mitchell's project?" Marion entered the back seat of her car and pushed the button that lowered the window.

"We've been meeting for late suppers the last few nights to share progress reports. He relishes every day on the job, feels he's contributing a little, and learning a great deal. He's an eternal optimist, and has all the necessary confidence and persistence to make such an enormous undertaking successful. I can't imagine Mitch not feeling fortunate to have him in the program."

Marion studied her face openly. "Douglas has been in love with you for some time now, hasn't he? Have you told him of your feelings for Mitchell?"

Brit considered her reply carefully. "He knows I'm not in love with him, and suspects there's something between Mitch and myself. I haven't wanted to say anything that could be misconstrued, and jeopardize his relationship with Mitch. You know Doug. He's always been protective of me."

"Yes, he's a dear, dear man. I hope he meets someone special, and right for him, soon."

"Maybe you could instigate a little matchmaking on his behalf, too. His conversation has been peppered with the name of a certain lady architect working with him. He seems to admire a Georgina Warren. Who knows—she might be unattached."

"What an inspired idea, Brittany." Marion lit up like a child receiving a surprise gift. "I'll speak with Doug later today. I'm off now to pick up the bedspreads and draperies, and then I go on to those darling antique stores over on Union Street between Gough and Steiner." She motioned to Soo Ling that she was ready to leave, and waved cheerily. "Pray without ceasing, my darling child, and then believe God will move mountains, if necessary, to provide the answer. I'll do everything I can to help Him."

Brittany plunged into her work with all her energy. If the kitchen and three prescribed bedrooms and baths were to be ready for their occupants in less than one week, there was no time to waste in moody contemplation of her future life with, or without, Mitchell Newmann. It would be difficult enough for his mother and daughter to live in the midst of daily construction, paint fumes, and pervasive plaster dust for the remainder of the summer, without having at least one cozy retreat apiece.

There were several surprises to show Mitchell on his next visit. Every few days during the month of labor, she or the workmen had unearthed buried treasure that revealed more about the origins of the house. Behind an ugly plywood panel in the kitchen, they had discovered a marvelous old brick fireplace. It had been made operative again, cleaned of layer upon layer of soot and grime, and scraped clean of several coats of paint. Marion had located an original cast iron soup pot to suspend from the rack in one corner of the hearth, and two lovely eighteenth-century oak rocking chairs to encourage enjoyment of its homeyness.

Brittany had used the charm of the fireplace, easily the center of attraction in the spacious kitchen, to set the tone of the remaining renovation in that area of the house. In keeping with the period, she had ordered a new electric stove with self-cleaning ovens housed in the shape and character of an old wood-burning range. She had removed layers of decayed linoleum from the floor, and now the original wide pine planks gleamed a soft shade of cinnamon under a protective coating of polyurethane.

On her daily rounds with Joe Vandervelde, at the end of the day, she presented a list of small details needing attention before the final cleanup and furniture delivery. "The knobs must be installed on the cupboards and drawers in the kitchen tomorrow, Joe.

Mrs. Stanford has located a cook and a housekeeper for me, and they need time to write out and fill orders for kitchen equipment and a stock of food. Have one of the men plug in the refrigerator, and make sure the ice maker is working. I noticed the drier in the laundry room is still without an exhaust hose and lint trap. The window in the master bedroom doesn't close all the way. Check to see if the culprit is new paint, or whether it should be rehung."

"It needs to be rehung. We have it on the schedule for tomorrow morning."

"How about the wallpaper in the room off Mrs. Newmann's suite? What's the holdup?"

"The first batch of that particular pattern was printed off-center on the paper. We had to send for a new supply. My hangers are right on top of things. They'll be out of there in two days. Don't worry, little lady, we won't let you down."

"I know you won't, Joe. Everyone has been absolutely super all month. It's not me I'm thinking of, but Mrs. Newmann and her young granddaughter. They'll both be unhappy about leaving their friends and a home they love. I want them to feel welcome here, and have a beautiful and peaceful retreat in the midst of all this chaos."

"They'll have it, if we all have to work until midnight the rest of the week, Miss Lawson. You have my word on that." He looked sideways at her, taking in the circles under her expressive eyes. "I sure do admire your tireless drive to do more than your share in spite of physical fatigue. I've never met another person who works any harder than you do. How are you doing on your football homework, by the way?"

Brit stopped to lean against the gracefully-turned banister of the sweeping stairway, and sighed happily. "Thanks to your son, I'm well on my way to becoming the most informed female in the city on the subject." Brittany playfully jabbed him in the ribs and bragged, "Ask me anything. If I can't give the right answer, I'll bake you one of my famous chocolate cakes with real fudge frosting."

Joe laughed. "Now, a man would be a fool to turn down an offer like that." He gazed upward at the ceiling in studied contemplation, twirling the unlit cigar in his mouth. "Let's see, now. Let's start with some basic facts. What's the size of a playing field, and what's that field called?"

"The *gridiron* is 300 feet long and 160 feet wide. It's divided into ten-yard divisions with white lines. At each end of the field are goal lines and goalposts."

"Hmm, you sound pretty confident. How many men are there on a team and how long is a game?" Joe removed the cigar and studied the cold gray ash at one end.

"There are eleven men per playing team—seven linemen and four others in the backfield. College and professional teams have both an offense and a defense team. The game consists of two thirty-minute halves, and each is divided into two fifteen-minute quarters."

Brit rattled off the information, standing at attention in front of her amused interrogator. Her dark eyes snapped with the stimulation of the challenge.

Joe grinned and met the goodnatured fray with equal enthusiasm. "What are the simple mechanics of the game, smarty?"

"The team with the ball wants to get a touchdown. This occurs when they carry or pass the ball over the other team's goal line. They have four chances to move the ball forward ten yards. The chances are called downs. Each time they succeed in making those ten yards, they are given four more chances, or downs, to move ten more yards."

"What happens if they don't make ten yards in four tries?"

"The other team gets the ball."

"So far, so good, little lady. But I'm getting hungry for that cake." Joe's eyes narrowed. "How many points for a touchdown?"

"Six."

"Is that the only way to make a score?"

"No. After a touchdown, the team has one more chance to make points. It can use a man called a kicker, who tries to get the ball over the crossbar between the goalposts for one point; or it can try to run or pass the ball over the goal line again for two extra points. Uh-uh-uh, Joe, don't interrupt me now! I'm not through." Brittany held up her hand to ward off his attempt to triumph, and rushed on with her recitation.

"A team can also score by making a field goal. If they're close to the goal line, but have failed to make those necessary ten yards after three downs, they can send in that kicker again on the fourth down. If he gets that ball over the crossbar—this time without first making a touchdown—it counts three points! Don't stop me, Joe, I'm on a roll. And, one more way. If a player with the ball is tackled down behind his own team's goal line, the other team gets two points. That infamous score is called a safety." Brit stopped when she ran out of breath, and preened saucily. "Now, you were saying?"

"You're getting cocky, Miss Lawson, but pride cometh before a fall. What are the officials called who oversee the game?"

"Referees."

"Can a team be punished?"

"Really, Joe, is that the best question you could come up with? Of course they can be. Football is rough. There are rules to follow, my dear man. If a rule gets broken by either team, the referee takes from five to fifteen yards away from them. Let's see, there's a penalty for holding, for interference, for being offside, for pulling the facemask off an opponent

. . . . Should I tell you exactly what each of those are?"

Brit batted her lashes and taunted Joe with a wide-toothed grin.

"Naw, you've got that stuff down cold." Joe chuckled and stuffed the cigar into one cheek. "Is that cake made from scratch or from a box mix?"

"From scratch, Mr. Vandervelde, and it's so moist and sinfuly rich, you'll feel like a criminal while reaching for a second and third piece."

"That good, eh? Guess I have to get rough, then. What's the place called where the two teams face off for each down?"

"The line of scrimmage."

"Who decides what play to use in each down?"

"The coach or the quarterback."

"What do the players discuss in the huddle before each play?"

"The quarterback gives the players a sequence of instructions. The information consists of the formation they will use, the number of the play itself, the onside linemen blocking combination, the backfield blocking assignment, the offside linemen blocking direction, and the count the quarterback will use. It's all done in one-syllable codes, like Full Right 18 Odd Bob 0 on l."

Brittany barked out the call like a pro, ending with a dramatic *hut-hut-hut*.

Joe collapsed against the stair rail and roared his approval. "By George, you have been doing your homework, gal! You've got me stumped. I can't think of another question."

"Oh, come on, Joe. Don't give up. Ask me some more."

"Nope. You've won, fair and square. I'm going to go home and cry in private over losing that cake." Joe started down the stairs, shaking his head. "This is a first for me."

Before he reached the last step, Brittany leaned over the banister for one more taunt. "Don't give up, Joe. I want you to get your reward."

"And I'd like that little prize you're tempting me with, gal, but I've decided you're too good for me," he rebutted, turning to wave his cigar at her.

"That's the best decision you've ever made, mister!"

Brittany's hands gripped the banister until their knuckles showed white boney ridges. How long had Mitch Newmann been in the house? He must have come in through the kitchen entry. If looks could kill a man, Joe Vandervelde would be on the floor. She had never seen Mitch so angry. His face was rigid with icy contempt.

"Mr. Newmann!" she cried, swallowing an hysterical laugh, and beginning a rapid descent of the steps. He must have heard the tail-end of their conversation and misinterpreted their intentions. "You're just the man I wanted to see." She struggled to keep her voice light.

Mitch's eyes transferred to her, and she knew he was taking in the excited flush on her face that her playful game with Joe had put there. There was a white line of tension around his nose, and a cynical twist to his lips.

"I'm not interrupting anything too personal, Miss Lawson?"

"No, not at all," she denied, darting an uneasy look in Joe's direction to see how he was taking Mitch's hostility. "We were only having a little . . . contest."

"I gathered that, and you were tempting Mr. Vandervelde with a prize?" Mitch's voice was deathly quiet, but his meaning was clear.

"Mr. Newmann?" Joe's cordial voice broke the tension between them. "I'm mighty glad to have this opportunity to meet you in person. Miss Lawson told me what you're planning to do for my boy, and I can't

144

tell you how pleased he'll be. Why, just having your autograph on a piece of scratch paper would have been enough to put stars in his eyes.''

A flicker of surprise appeared in Mitch's eyes, intermingled with confusion. He delayed extending his hand to meet Joe's, long enough to exchange a quick glance with Brittany again. She appealed to him with a movement from her eyebrows, and he made the obligatory handshake with customary politeness.

"Thank you for those kind words. I'm not the celebrity your son is really interested in, however, so I took the liberty of asking for the signatures of a few players. If you'll look in on the front seat of my car on your way out, you'll find a signed football there, and a package containing a few Forty-Niner's souvenirs. I also asked my secretary to enclose a couple tickets to the first pre-season game in August. If I had a son, I would want to do the same as you. Tell him the whole team wishes him a happy birthday.''

The look on Joe's face was so touching, Brittany had to turn away in order to hide the gathering moisture clouding her vision. She heard him clear his throat and thank Mitch with a gruff acceptance of the unexpected bonanza of gifts. At the door, he turned, his lapse in poise under control.

"I'll tell you who should *really* have that stuff, sir— this lady architect of yours. She's a football wizard! It beats me why some guy hasn't snapped her up long ago. She would make the best dad-gummed wife a sports loving man could ever hope to have. Imagine having a wife *eager* to watch a game with you, and then *understanding* every dad-gummed minute of it! A man couldn't do enough for a gal like that, especially if she were half as gorgeous as Miss Lawson there. Well, thanks again, sir. See you tomorrow, Miss Lawson.''

"Wait, Joe!" Brittany called, halting him at the door.

"Yes, ma'am?"

"You just earned yourself that cake we talked about."

"I did, huh?" Joe shifted the soggy cigar with his tongue and grinned crookedly. "I don't suppose we could frost it with a *double* batch of that homemade fudge!"

"Absolutely not! It would make you sick."

"Have I earned any sick leave?"

"Get out of here, Joe. Don't press your luck."

Brittany shoved him out the door with a bubble of laughter, and closed it firmly. She was alone with Mitch again after two weeks. This was her golden opportunity to confess ignorance of his wife's death at the time she fled Baltimore.

It took a conscious effort to face him, but she did, and then flinched inwardly at the dark disdain visible on his face. "I want to know what that was all about, Brittany!" he demanded through clenched teeth.

"There's nothing to know, Mitch," she shrugged, trying to appear nonchalant under his close scrutiny.

"I think there is," he insisted. "That little scene could hardly be classified a business conference."

Brittany's mouth curved upward into a smile wide enough to create dimples. "Not *your* style business, perhaps. I can't quite picture you making payments with chocolate cakes."

Mitch's grey eyes narrowed in confused speculation. "I'm in no mood for games, Brit. If Vandervelde is making demands on you for favors, whether they are cakes, or something more personal, I want to know about it." The glitter in his eyes shone like the polished steel of daggers.

"You are jumping to conclusions again," she accused, secretly pleased with his reaction. Was he jealous of her easy relationship with his foreman? Tilting her head to peer up at him through a thick fringe of lashes, she challenged, "Would you believe a

146

homemade cake was the payoff on a friendly wager over football?''

Mitch's mouth thinned. "You'd better explain."

"Sure. Joe fancies himself an expert on football, and I challenged him to a duel, of sorts. I'm quite knowledgeable myself, you know." He didn't need to know her expertise was newly acquired and for his benefit, that she loved him so much that she would watch football for the rest of her life to please him. Was this what Lewis meant by coming in the back door? She eyed Mitch coquettishly. "I bet Joe a cake if he could stump me."

"And did he?" Mitch's low voice reflected his disbelief.

"Actually, he didn't," Brittany laughed softly. "I decided to give him the cake anyway, for saying such nice things about me. I'm a soft touch when my ego is stroked." She laughed again, and strode forward to link her arm through his. "You should try it sometime, Mitch." She gave him a sidelong glance. "Believe me?"

He studied her face with comment.

"Ask me something. I'll prove it," she prodded, nudging him gently with an elbow to his ribs. "I'll betcha another batch of homemade American fries you can't outwit me. Okay?''

Brittany moistened her lips with a tentative tongue before spreading them into a kittenish smile. "Come on, Mitch. I dare you. Ask me anything you want about the Forty-Niners—about the players, the positions they play, their standings in the National Football League, the records they've made—anything. Do you know who the new owner of the team is?''

She caught her full bottom lip under her upper teeth, and laughed at him with deeply dark, onyx eyes. Was this what Marion meant by stoking the fire?

"You're crazy, do you know that?" Mitch's arm

relaxed under her tight grip, and the warmth of his smile reached his eyes, melting the ice and revealing once again the sense of humor she loved.

Nodding coyly, she pressed her cheek against his shoulder. "That's what you've always told me."

Lowering his face, Mitch kissed her softly and quickly on the lips. "You're full of surprises, Gypsy. I didn't know you liked football."

"It takes time to know everything about a person, Mitch," she responded quietly, her voice thick with unspoken love. "For example, I didn't know you were a widower until this month."

CHAPTER 9

BRITTANY SENSED MITCH'S WITHDRAWAL even before she saw the curtain come down over his eyes. She dropped the issue immediately, and lightheartedly grasped his hand, tugging on it with a surge of ebullience.

"Did you see the surprise in the kitchen, Mitch? Isn't it lovely? I had one of the workmen remove a hideous plywood panel tacked up to hold utensils, and intended to replace it with another section of cupboards, but he discovered something far more important."

She pulled him to the threshold of the kitchen and stopped her chattering with a smile of immense pleasure. "Isn't it wonderful, Mitch? We removed layers of paint and soot, but every brick is an original. Can't you picture Hally warming in front of a blazing fire after school, and munching on home-baked cookies? Did you notice the high-beamed ceiling? We took down those frosted, plastic panels hiding a series of fluorescent lights, and found it. Marion thinks we should have a ceiling fan. What do you think?"

She finally risked a glance in his direction, her eyes bright with inquiry. His returning look was disturbingly direct, but completely devoid of emotion. Feeling her spirits dip, she went on hurriedly, not waiting for a reply. "A fan might be the perfect solution for days when the central air conditioners aren't running. I know a shop with a large collection of reconditioned originals. Look at the ceiling itself. I used recessed lights between the beams in order to retain authenticity as much as possible. One or two small chandeliers would provide too little light, I think."

She slanted him another look, but this time he was examining the kitchen with a practiced eye. "The natural ceiling is magnificent. It gives a nice feeling of space. I'm glad you used recessed lights; they provide the correct amount of incandescence in the exact place of need. I agree with you and Marion about the fan, but it might be wiser to buy a reproduction rather than an antique. The new fans have variable speeds and a reverse switch to direct the draft upward. This makes it useable in winter months to recirculate the warm air trapped near the ceiling, and it also prevents flour from blowing off the counters when someone is cooking."

Brittany basked in the warmth and joy filling her heart. The nail-breaking hard work she had expended was quickly forgotten with Mitch's praise. How lucky for her that she had stayed late with Joe. She wouldn't give up this private moment with Mitch for anything. How she loved seeing his interest and pleasure.

She watched him roam the kitchen, touch cabinets and doors with knowledgeable hands, and examine the bricks and flue of the fireplace with an eye for both beauty and function. "I haven't had an opportunity to discuss this with you before now, Mitch, but the Stanford's housekeeper has found a wonderful Oriental couple, who meet her strict standards, for a possible cook and groundkeeper. She also gave me the name of a housekeeper and a part-time maid. I've already interviewed them and feel you would be happy with their service and personalities. If they don't prove satisfactory, you could replace them after you and your family are settled and have more time to devote to a search."

"You're really something, Brit. Thank you," he said, rewarding her with an all-too-rare smile. "To be honest, I never gave a minute's thought to hiring a staff, and we'll need them all. My mother has always done for herself, but the old family home is much smaller than this place. As you already know, she won't be able to work from now on."

Encouraged by his friendly tone of voice, and his easy acceptance of her efforts on his behalf, Brittany became even more eager to show him other parts of the house. "Come on, Mitch. Give me your opinions on a couple other projects we've initiated." Unable to check her enthusiasm, she flashed her dimpled cheeks and preceded him back through the breakfast room, dining room, and into the central hall.

"Marion adores this special project of mine, Mitch, and I honestly believe it was a stroke of genius on my part to have thought of it." She laughed gleefully, and waited for him to catch up with her, finally lacing her fingers with his. "Come on, slowpoke! It's at the end of the hall near the garden room."

The laughter in his glinting eyes, and a heartwarming smile that softened the hard plains of his face, made Brit's pulse clamor in double time. If only she could throw herself into his arms and convince him of her undying love, everything would be perfect.

"Mitchell, darling, there you are!" Alexis Seifert's unmistakable voice stopped them both dead in their tracks. "When I couldn't reach you anywhere, I knew you must have come to make an inspection of the house."

Brittany yanked her hand from Mitch's and balled it

151

into a tight fist. She could hardly refrain from kicking the wall in her frustration, but pivoted slowly to watch him greet his lovely woman at the front door where she posed with a sickeningly sweet smile.

"I'm not late for the meeting, am I, Alexis?" Mitch made a hasty inspection of his watch.

"No, of course not, dear, but I found that information you needed, and thought you would want to look it over before we meet with Reverend Katkov tonight. It seemed important to you and you already know what it means to me." She brushed a long, black hair from his shoulder and allowed her fragile fingers to linger possessively.

Brit's spirits plummeted. Alexis was taking no chances on losing Mitch. She had already initiated wedding plans. They were meeting with the minister.

"You're incredible, Alexis. What would I do without you? You are able to anticipate my needs and provide solutions before I even have time to think of them. You're wonderful."

Alexis laughed charmingly. "It's my job to make matters go smoothly for you, Mitchell." She dashed a quick peek in Brittany's direction. "Are you through here, darling?"

Mitch turned before Brittany could avert her face, and the slight raising of his eyebrows indicated he had seen the naked jealousy in her eyes. As though digesting her reaction, he hesitated before answering Alexis's question. "Not quite," he said, his look holding Brit's through sheer force of will.

"Miss Lawson had a few more things to show me concerning the restoration work. Why don't you stay, and then I'll follow you over to Reverend Katkov's office." He drew her forward with a hand on her elbow.

"What an excellent idea, darling. I haven't had a free second to stop by and check on the progress this week. We'll have to make it a rather hurried tour, though, Miss Lawson," she added with an apologetic purr. "Tonight's meeting is one Mitch and I want to make on time."

"I know what you mean," Brit returned dramatically. Not to be outwitted, she took a studied look at her watch, and made a grimace. "I'm running short of time myself, and Doug will have fits if I'm late. We can make it, I guess, if we really push." Without waiting for a reply, she headed down the hall, her head held high, her long dark hair cascading down her back.

Avoiding piles of building debris stacked into piles along the passageway, she stopped before a cage of ornate grillwork encased in mirrors and glass.

"Good heavens!" mumbled Alexis, overworking her eyebrows. "What is this monstrosity?" She picked her way past Brittany and examined the area with a pained expression, throwing disparaging looks at Mitch over her shoulder.

"It's an elevator, *obviously*," Brittany replied facetiously. Ignoring Alexis, she sought Mitch's attention and recited a polite, but defensively chilly explanation. "I put the elevator here for your mother's use. Some people with severe angina find it difficult to climb stairs, and without a better means of moving about such a large house, she would become a virtual prisoner in her room. I chose this style, rather than an elevator hidden in some closet, for the very reason that it's not hidden. If some problem should develop with your mother or the elevator, other members of the household can see at a glance if the elevator is occupied. It's large enough to hold a wheel chair if one becomes necessary, and it can be operated quite easily without a second person."

Unaccountable tears welled in her eyes, and she quickly averted her face, pretending to inspect the conveyance. "If you find this an unnecessary encumbrance, it can be removed."

"Miss Lawson doesn't seem to understand that matters as costly as this should be discussed *before* they're undertaken, Mitch. All this expense could have been avoided. San Francisco has several exceedingly competent nursing homes for elderly citizens needing special attention. I'm on the board of one especially fine establishment, and my grandmother has been a resident there for several years." Alexis' voice had taken on the tone of a teacher instructing an ignorant child. "Most old people today don't want to be a burden to their families."

"Since when are a mother's needs burdens?" Brittany mumbled to herself.

"Pardon me?"

Brit bit back a sharp retort with tightly compressed lips, and glowered at Mitch, expecting him to refute Alexis' callous disregard for his parent—her future mother-in-law—but for some reason he was pretending he hadn't heard. "Is the elevator functioning now, Miss Lawson?" he asked curtly, not even bothering to look in her direction while addressing her.

"Yes, of course it is!" Her response was automatic and sharpened by a rapidly rising anger. Mitch had always accused her of having a short fuse, so it should come as no surprise to him that she resented interference from Alexis. He had promised her a free hand, and he knew very well his fiancée's perceptions of things were at variance with her own. Evidently, he was blind to her faults already.

"Why don't we take a ride to the second floor then," he suggested, opening the door and motioning for her to enter. "We can test it and kill two birds with one stone."

Brittany sucked in the sides of her cheeks and heaved an impatient sigh. With clenched fists, she marched past Mitch and stood stiffly at the rear of the suddenly miniature enclosure. She avoided meeting his gaze, and concentrated on the floor.

When Alexis crossed into the space in front of her, bringing the cloying scent of her floral perfume, Brit made a childish sniff and covered her nose with one hand.

"Here we are, ladies. Watch your step, please." The deep timbre of Mitch's voice carried a strong hint of amusement, but when Brittany strode past him and snatched a sidelong peek through the lowered hood of her lashes, his look was enigmatic.

"What else did you want to show us, Miss Lawson?" he asked, his voice strictly businesslike again. His hand rested on Alexis' waist this time, an effective reminder of the woman's place in his life.

Brittany shook her head helplessly, fighting for poise in the face of his betrayal of her and of his own principles. "Nothing in particular," she said stiffly. 'Why don't you look over the bedrooms on your own. If you have any questions, I'll do my best to provide answers. Your mother's rooms are here to the right, your daughter's are in the front wing across from the master bedroom suite."

Alexis lost no time finding something to ridicule. With chilling disdain, she enumerated her objections. "Look at this room, Mitchell. Who are you using for an interior decorator, Miss Lawson? Methuselah? This room is a disaster! Rocking chairs, lace doilies, piece quilts, lace curtains . . .*really!* This room belongs in a museum, not in the home of a prominent, contemporary architect. And what is all this?"

She had opened a door leading into a small alcove, with another door at the far end entering a second, slightly smaller bedroom. The alcove contained a compact cooking center with a two-burner stove topping a small refrigerator, and a microwave oven installed overhead. Next to it, a mini-sink and cupboard held a set of lovely old china.

It was unduly quiet in the bedroom with Alexis in the next room. Mitchell was still mute after her harangue. Brittany decided to brazen it out with him. If he wanted changes to please his fiancée there would be only a few more days in which to make them before his mother arrived.

Heaving a sigh of exasperation, Brittany plunged into her explanation. "I'm sure you recognize many of your mother's personal belongings, Mitch. If Marion and I misunderstood your intentions for their use, we apologize. We wanted to make this room restful and familiar, a welcome retreat for your mother, to ease the pain of leaving her home. We thought her things would bring her comfort and a sense of continuity. I chose this room for her because it was unusually large, and could be divided into several areas, including one for sleeping and one for lounging around the fireplace. Over here, Marion is planning to put a game table for cards or jigsaw puzzles. The large corner windows look out onto the beautiful gardens, and the pool. She can sit there and enjoy the out-of-doors on days when she isn't up to leaving her room or dressing."

Mitch walked to the windows and looked out. Brittany stopped speaking to catch her breath, and watched him with pounding temples. His face was made of granite. Did he like it or not? Why didn't he say something? What had happened to the camaraderie they had shared in the kitchen not ten minutes ago?

"I suppose it was presumptuous of me to do all this without your approval, but I did ask for your help, Mitch. You might as well hear everything I've done now, and then if you want to dismiss me, you may. I arranged a passageway into the adjoining bedroom in case you want to hire a companion-nurse for your mother. There's easy communication and movement between rooms when the doors are left ajar during times of greatest need. The compact kitchen will allow your mother independence from your private life. She can prepare herself simple favorite meals or indulge in a midnight snack without disturbing the household."

She was rambling on and on, and it was shattering her nerves. How much longer could she endure his silence?

Mitch pivoted suddenly, and his eyes probed hers with such intensity it set her heart pounding like Indian drums during a rain dance. A pulse jerked at his temple at the same insane speed.

In a nervous gesture, she ran her fingers through the thick lock of hair that tended to fall over one eye, and attempted to push it behind her ear. Her entire hand was shaking, and she was certain her discomfort and anxiety showed in her face. It angered her that she had so little control over herself around Mitch— especially at times like this when she was actively seeking his approval and was so openly vulnerable to criticism from him. He claimed he could read her like a book, and yet he was too blind to see that she loved him, and needed his forgiveness. Why didn't he speak? Was he so disappointed in her work he was at a loss for words?

Alexis came clicking back into the room, her high-heeled shoes tapping a sharp staccato. Before she could say another word, Brittany jumped in with a hastily-concocted story. "I hope you folks will excuse me, but I've got to run. I have an important date to keep, and I'm completely out of time. Don't forget to turn off the lights and lock up the house when you leave."

Ignoring the deep scowl on Mitch's face, she backed out of the door in mid-sentence, and sped down the long hallway toward the central staircase. Before her long strides removed her from earshot, she heard Alexis' despicable voice. "It's shocking to be treated with such rude behavior by a so-called professional, Mitchell darling. You shouldn't tolerate it. At the very least, she should be reported to Lewis. He can't afford to have his firm's reputation ruined by such discourteous representatives."

Brittany flicked back the stray lock of hair with angry fingers, and took the stairs two at a time. She wasn't interested in waiting for Mitchell's reply, but it didn't take a genius to figure it out. He had changed. He wasn't the fair-minded, honorable, straight forward, kind gentleman she had known.

Was she responsible? Had her unfair desertion in Baltimore made him bitter and distrustful? Had he lost all respect for her honesty and integrity? With what great pleasure he must have savored the passionate expression of her deep love! It had given him the perfect opportunity to fling it back in her face.

She deserved the pain he was inflicting upon her. How could she fault him for returning her treatment of him? He must hate her as deeply as he had once professed to love her.

Suffused by her anguish, Brittany stumbled into her car and searched blindly through the purse, hastily pulled from under the seat, for her keys. Her chest heaved as she drew long, hard breaths through pinched nostrils. Finally, she gave up and collapsed over the steering wheel, sobbing silently with tight lips and dry eyes.

God help her, in spite of anything Mitch might say or do, she loved him. Her love was an indisputable fact, but somehow, she had to muster enough self-respect to refuse any more punishment.

A sigh broke from her, and with it a prayer for resignation and the renewed strength to go on with her life. It began with the simple activity of locating her keys, inserting the correct one into the ignition, and driving through the darkened streets of the city to her apartment.

Love was a mysterious emotion. It seemed to be invincible against all manners of reason. It certainly had nothing to do with common sense. But in the end, if she truly loved Mitch, then his happiness should be paramount. If he loved Alexis—and love *must* be blind if that were true—then, she should rejoice for him and let him go.

Everything about Mitch was stored away in her heart and memory, anyhow. She had never forgotten how his smile would flash without warning, illuminating the soft gray of his eyes with dancing lights. She knew every clean-cut line of his face, had traced them with her fingers numerous times when simply touching him was important to her sanity. She could never forget the contagious sound of his laughter, or the husky breaks in his deep voice when he called her his beautiful gypsy, and whispered words of love.

Lord, thank You for allowing me the privilege of knowing Mitch's love for even a short time. Thank You for showing me the importance of trust in a relationship. Yours is the only perfect love, Lord, and I'm beginning to understand You might have used this painful experience with Mitch to draw me closer to You. I have finally learned to put You first in my life, at least most of the time, but I still need to trust You to provide for my future. It won't be easy to give up hope for a life with Mitch, but I can do it with Your help. I'm going to need plenty of it, though. Mitch is special, Lord. He won't be easy to forget.

Brittany's apartment seemed unusually small, cold, and empty when she closed the door behind her. The silence had never bothered her before, but now, it seemed to grow like a viable presence, and she could feel it pinning her against the wall.

Numb and lethargic, she wanted nothing more than to give in to the insidious depression taking over her will to even move. Had Mitch felt like this when he returned from his site visit to find her gone? Had he felt like a hollowed-out shell, with his very life torn from him?

Brit gazed bleakly around the room. This was her home. Casebolt House was merely a job—one small part of her life—one that tested her talent and

159

expertise and that paid her well. There would be many others like it in her long, lonely future.

Somehow she found the strength to move, and snapped on the stereo radio, switching the station deliberately from soft mood music, to loud hard rock. The strident sounds abraded her senses, but they also made thinking impossible.

Minutes later, she was in the kitchen preparing Joe Vandervelde's chocolate cake, dressed in a comfortable velour jogging suit of vivid Oriental red, the bright color and the frenzied music removed her from the world of dark foreboding. Shunning the electric mixer on the counter, she aggressively beat the cake batter with a large wooden spoon. For the first time, she understood why her grandmother proclaimed there was no better method of problem-solving than baking a cake or scrubbing a floor.

If making one cake could ease her present state of mind, then a second one should soon have her back to normal. Brit attacked the second batch of batter with even greater intensity, whipping the spoon through the dark batter again and again until her arm ached. After cooking the fudge frosting, she washed the dishes by hand, drying each piece with meticulous care. When she put them away, she took time to straighten all the drawers and cupboards. With that chore finished, she chopped walnuts, one at a time with a short paring knife.

At the end of an hour and a half, she was climbing walls. The cakes were frosted and decorated, the kitchen was spotless, and the loud abrasive music was finally setting her teeth on edge.

Marching back to the living room, she switched stations on the radio to a baseball game. The impersonal voice of the announcer filled the room with human sound, but this time, it was calming. It could even be ignored.

A sharp pattern of knocks startled her, and with her

heart in her throat, she pulled open the door without waiting to peek through the hidden eye. "Doug, *darling!*" she cried, drawing him into the apartment with eager hands. "How did you know I had just baked a cake and was wishing you were here to share it?"

His look was more than quizzical. Her enthusiasm bordered on hysteria. "What's wrong, Brit?" he asked.

"Wrong? What in the world could be wrong? Didn't you hear me? I said I've baked a cake, and want to have a. . .a p-party!" Her breath caught in her throat.

"Okay, fine, I'm all for it." Doug grinned, one of his endearingly quaint traits, and held out his arms. "How about a welcome hug for your *darling* before we celebrate?"

Brittany felt her chin wobble in response to his kindly, welcome voice. She needed a shoulder to lean on, and arms to comfort her. She needed him . . . good old, dependable Doug.

His hands came up to pull her forward. "Come on, gal," he encouraged, quietly wrapping his arms around her and swaying in the rhythmic movement associated with a mother consoling her child.

"Do you know how many times I've wanted to hold you here, Brit?" He touched his lips to her forehead and rested his freckled cheek against the top of her hair. "I should be tap-dancing on the ceiling, but somehow the sight of unshed tears shimmering over those bewitchingly dark eyes of yours has brought out the brotherly instinct in me instead. Can you imagine that? After five years of patient pursuit, you fall into my arms, and all I want to do is kiss your hurt and make it well."

"Poor Doug." Brit's voice was muffled against his chest. Why couldn't she love him? He was so incredibly . . . what? Understanding.

"Let's not waste any compassion on me, pal. I

161

want to know what's happened to turn you from a calm, confident associate, into a pale, harried basket-case.''

Brit stirred restlessly, wishing he would just hold her and not expect anything in return. His arms tightened until she grunted a protest. "I know the cat didn't get that tongue of yours. If I have to squeeze the information out of you, I will, Brit, and I absolutely refuse to eat your cake without it." He applied more pressure. "Say, 'okay, Uncle Doug,' and I'll stop crunching you."

"You're crazy," Brit protested through her teeth. Her lips were flattened against his shirt.

"I can't hear you!"

"Okay, Uncle Doug!"

His arms slackened. "That's what I like . . . willful cooperation." His keen, green eyes searched her face. "What's up, Brit? You've been wasting away, growing thinner and paler by the day this month. It's because of Mitch Newmann, isn't it?"

Brit summoned a weak smile and pushed him away. "I thought I had finally gained a brother, and it seems I have a private psychiatrist."

"Ouch. That hurts. I'm not going to even look at the cake now, not until you apologize. If nothing else, I'm your good friend and deserve a thank-you for my loving concern for your health."

"I'm sorry if you feel slighted, Doug. I didn't mean it in a derogatory way." She patted his cheek and smiled tremulously. "You're a true-blue pal, you know that? And now that I know that you know we're only friends and nothing more—in a romantic sense— I've just got to do something." With the index fingers of both hands, she smoothed back the helter-skelter bushiness of his carrot-red eyebrows. "I've been dying to do that ever since I first met you, Mr. Kennedy."

His grin widened while he shook his head. "There's

no question about it, you're as nutty as a fruitcake.'' Taking hold of her wrists, he pulled her toward the kitchen, stopping to turn off the stereo. ''I know I shouldn't give in so easily, but the smell of that fudge is making me weak. What's with all this interest in football and baseball? As if I didn't know. You're in love with Mitch Newmann, aren't you, Brit? And Mitch Newmann owns a football team.''

Brit skipped a beat to match his stride, and felt her own resolve weaken. It was time to be honest with Doug. ''Yes, I am—irrevocably, hopelessly, helplessly, and all the other ways imaginable.''

''Sounds like the real thing, all right. Look at those cakes! Which one is mine?''

''Neither one is *yours*, mister. I'll give you a slice of one, *if* you behave yourself. Go and sit down. You're being a pest.'' Brit pointed across the narrow kitchen at the two stools.

''Yes, ma'am. So, tell me now, if you love Mitch, and he loves you, why are you so unhappy? The circles under your eyes remind me of the basset hound I had as a kid.'' Doug straddled a stool and entwined his hands behind his head.

''You have such a lovely way of expressing yourself,'' Brit retorted, finding comfort in the offhanded banter. She reached for two plates from a cupboard. ''The problem is, you don't know what you're talking about. Mitch in no way shares my sentiments.''

''That's not the impression he gives me.''

''What are you talking about now, Doug?''

''Mitch. He asks me about you whenever we work together on the new project—not in so many words, but the conversation is always maneuvered to get your name introduced. It's pretty obvious to me he's jealous of our relationship, and wants to know exactly how involved it is.''

Brit placed the dishes on the counter next to the cake and paused to ruffle Doug's mop of thick red hair. "You're blind as a bat, my pet brother. You've focused on the wrong lady. Your fellow architect and new boss is already engaged and ready to tie the matrimonial knot."

"I don't believe it. Who's the dame?"

"Get your fingers off the frosting. His future mistress of Casebolt House is none other than the exquisite Alexis Seifert, former widow of Joseph Chapman, and former wife of Karl M. Seifert, the third."

Doug's spontaneous laughter filled the room.

"Go ahead and laugh if you want to. It's the truth, and . . . and the truth . . . hurts!" Brit glared at him, her hands on her hips.

"Oh, come on, Brit, you don't believe that! The man's not blind. The dear gal is older than he is and not at all his type."

"She's also rich and well-known, a part of the San Francisco establishment. She calls him 'darling,' and they went to see the minister tonight."

"She calls me 'darling,' too."

"Haven't you seen her ring?"

"Which one? I have never seen her wear fewer than three."

Brittany opened her mouth to voice another comeback, but the doorbell interrupted. "That must be the paper boy on collection. Stay here, and keep your fingers off the cake until I return. It will only take a minute."

"Well, make it snappy. My patience is wearing thin."

"I love you, Doug. You're the best medicine I've ever had," she laughed, leaving him to run for the impatient door.

"*Mitch!*" Brit gaped at him and felt the color surge upward over her cheeks.

"You left in such a hurry, we couldn't finish our business." He was propped against the door frame with one hand, and looked so bone-tired, her heart went out to him. He searched her face, waiting for her response. Her lips parted, but no sounds came out, and she knew it was impossible to hide the effect he had on her. He was only one step away, but it seemed like miles.

He waited, and all she could do was speak to him with her own dark gaze. She loved the way he looked right now. Why did he have to make truthfulness between them so difficult? Had he been thinking about her revelation at Casebolt House? Did he understand, now, that she hadn't known he was a widower?

"Brit," he said finally, his voice a husky growl. He was breathing hard. So was she. He took the one step, gathering her to himself. His lips sank into the softness of her neck. Brittany pressed against him, and tried to speak of her love.

Why couldn't they sit close to each other and speak of all the mistakes they had made, and then forgive each other and share plans for a future? Why must the words stick in their throats?

"Hey, Brit! Hurry up out there. My patience is wearing thin. How long are you going to make me wait?"

At the first sound of Doug's voice, Mitch jerked away. His eyes smoldered with rage. "Is that Kennedy in there?" he snarled.

"Yes," Brit admitted, casting an aggravated look behind her. "He stopped by for . . ."

"I can imagine. Spare me the details. I don't need you to draw a picture for me."

"Mitch!" Brit's face became ashen with his ugly accusation. "How dare you speak to me like that! You have no right!"

"Thanks for reminding me." Mitch's lips twisted into a bitter curl. "You'd better get back to him before he decides to leave, too." He pivoted abruptly and strode down the hall to the elevators.

"Wait, Mitch, it isn't what you think!" Brit started after him on a run. She couldn't let him leave this time.

"Save your lies, lady. I've had enough of them."

"But, we haven't discussed Casebolt House yet. Don't go, Mitch. I'll tell Doug to leave. We can talk. We *need* to talk."

"I wouldn't think of interrupting, Miss Lawson. Had I known he was here, I wouldn't have stopped by at all. My intention was only to tell you I approve of your work at the house, and want to keep everything as it is." His face was stony, his voice cold.

Brittany saw only a blur, and for that brief moment his former words were forgotten. "Y—you like it?" she stammered, her voice shaky and hoarse with feeling.

There was no answer, and when her rapid blinking cleared her vision of the rush of happy tears, she saw that he was gone. Somehow, she made it back to her apartment and closed the door, leaning heavily against it.

"Brit, what's the hold-up?"

Rousing herself, she met Doug's inquisitive gaze. For the life of her, she couldn't provide a lighthearted answer. "It was Mitch."

"Why didn't you invite him in, gal? I wouldn't object to sharing my cake with him." He grinned and then sobered at the stricken look on her face. "Don't tell me. I can guess. Your lipstick is smudged from ear to ear, but you look ready for the grave. I spoke up at the wrong moment, huh?"

She nodded forlornly, and linked arms with him. "It wasn't your voice as much as what you said and how you said it."

"What I said?" Doug was clearly perplexed. "I merely reminded you I was ready. You mean he thinks you and I are an item?" Doug laughed convulsively and pinched her in the ribs. "He's jealous, sis. Your big brother speaketh the truth."

166

"At least he likes my work. He said I should keep everything as it is."

"Of course he likes it. That's one of the reasons he hired you. And in my brotherly wisdom, I ascertain the second reason was to keep his eye on you until he could make up his mind."

"About what?"

"About you. I want my cake before I give any more interpretations. Serve some to yourself at the same time. You know what Mary Poppins said. A spoonful of sugar makes the medicine go down."

Reluctantly Brit had to smile. "I wish you were my real brother, Doug; then you'd be around for the rest of my life."

"Consider it done."

While they ate the generous pieces of chocolate cake, and imbibed ice-cold milk, they chatted comfortably about their work. The conversation included the name Georgina several times, and finally Brit demanded an explanation. "If I'm made to bare my soul, Douglas, then you should reciprocate in kind. You're actually buttery whenever you use her name."

Doug examined his fork in detail before answering. "Do you still believe in love at first sight, Brit? Girls usually do when they're in their teens."

Brit controlled the twitching at the corner of her lips. This was no time to break into dimples. Doug was serious. "I'm not in my teens, but I don't think the phenomenon is limited to immature females, or males. Are you in love with Georgina?"

"If I'm not, then I have no good explanation for my feelings. Whereas I enjoy and look forward to being with you, I devise endless opportunities to catch even a glimpse of Georgie. I call her on the pretext of eliciting information about the project, and the questions I ask need such simple answers, she must be convinced by now I'm an ignorant nincompoop."

"You're in love all right. Oh, Doug, isn't it

wonderful?'' Brit hugged him in joyful exuberance. "I can't wait to meet her."

"You will, tomorrow evening at Lewis' birthday party for Marion. Mitch will be there, no doubt. Marion will see to that." He put down his fork and patted his stomach. "That's the best cake I've ever eaten. You'll have to give the recipe to Georgina." He rose from the stool and placed his hands on Brit's shoulders. "You're worrying for nothing, you know. Mitch Newmann is putting up resistance, but the die is cast. He keeps coming back for more, and one of these times, it will be for good. It's an honor for any man to be loved by you, honey. Sometimes a man's pride gets in the way of his surrender, that's all. We men resist changes of any kind. We prefer to believe we have total control over every minute of our lives. Anything less is a sign of weakness. Look at me. I've resisted marriage for thirty-one years, and now I'm ready to take the plunge at a second's notice."

He kissed her chastely on the cheek. "See you tomorrow, Brit."

"Wait a minute. I want to wrap up the rest of that cake for you to take home."

"But it isn't *mine*, Miss Lawson."

"It is, now."

168

CHAPTER 10

THE NEXT DAY, Brittany worked in a frenzy, and there was no opportunity to fret over the increased gulf between herself and Mitch. A steady parade of workmen, delivery people, and household staff kept her mind completely occupied.

Before the work day ended, the restorations had been concluded in three bedroom suites—including bathrooms, dressing areas and sitting rooms—the kitchen, laundry room, pantry, and breakfast room. The housekeeping staff had prepared lists of necessities and had presented them for approval, and a series of deliveries had filled the rooms with new and antique furniture, lamps, rugs, and accessories.

With Marion Stanford's help, the furniture would be properly arranged the next day. The new housekeeper and maid would wash windows, stock the bathrooms with linens, hang curtains and drapes, and make up beds. The new cook and her husband would shop for kitchen supplies and food, with Mrs. Chang along to supervise.

Brittany ran quick fingers through her tangled hair,

and wiped the film of perspiration from her forehead with the back of her hand. She was filthy and exhausted.

Joe joined her in the kitchen after the last workman had left the premises. "I told the crews not to return until Monday, Miss Lawson."

"Good. They deserve a few days of rest. You do, too. Joe, I can't begin to express my appreciation for the long hours you've put in this month. You kept everything going like clockwork, handling problems with such ease and finesse, you never missed a beat. I'm impressed—thrilled—with the quality work performed by each crew. The Newmanns will be, too. I can't wait to finish the rest of the house now, especially the exterior."

"I know what you mean. The craftsmanship in these old homes is unsurpassed, especially by today's slap-them-up-in-a-hurry standards. It's a kick working on a place like this."

"I feel the same way, Joe. I love the high ceilings, the graceful detailing and pleasing proportions. In this house, in particular, the interior space flows so smoothly from one area to another, it was easy to respect the original architecture and only attempt to update it tastefully."

Joe removed a new cigar from his mouth and shifted it into his left hand. "I'd like to shake your hand, if I could, Miss Lawson, and speak for all the crew members as well as myself. You're the first woman we've worked for that didn't throw daily tantrums and change her mind as often as the wind changes directions. You sure know what you're doing. You do your homework and we all appreciate that. I intend to tell Mr. Newmann he picked himself a humdinger when he hired you. There's something pretty special about the way you treat people. Makes them want to bend over backward to please you."

Brittany shook his hand with misting eyes. This was

a special part of what made her work worthwhile. The house itself was an unfinished skeleton. It might outlast several generations of its inhabitants, and become a monument to a particular epoch in time, but the people were more important to her. Every architect dreamed of making a lasting impression—a statement of his talent and theory that would live on as proof he existed. She shared the same dreams. But she found equal satisfaction in restoring the great beauty of the past for a new generation to not only enjoy and appreciate, but also to utilize.

"Thanks, Joe. You sure know how to make a person feel terrific."

"So do you. I've been sneaking samples of that fudge cake all day. I'm going to take it home now and share it with my family. If you need me for anything between now and Monday, give me a call. I can't wait to see my kid's face when he opens that box of Forty-Niners gifts from Mr. Newmann. This has been some week. One of the best ever."

Brittany watched Joe leave before gathering her portfolio of materials and the list of activities for the next day, and then heading for her own car. It would take at least two hours to make herself presentable for Marion Stanford's birthday party.

Two and a half hours later, she was bathed, shampooed, and dressed. A subtle barely-there blush of color highlighted her high cheekbones and made her look glowingly healthy. Her raven hair shimmered under the ceiling light, and the free-flowing style she preferred to wear made her look mysterious and, at the same time, earthy.

She chose to wear a tank-style, silk chemise in wild berry colors, with a matching kimono jacket. The light fabric draped her body and made her look and feel every bit a woman. It was a nice change after a day in dirty jeans and sneakers.

Parking her car behind a long line of others, and

walking the block and a half to the Stanford's, Brittany felt her trepidation grow. Mitch would be at the party. Would he talk to her? Should she set aside her pride and come right out and ask him if he was engaged to marry Alexis? Why did people find it so difficult to communicate with those they cared the most about, when they could discuss the most infinite details of any subject with a stranger?

Tense as a coiled spring, she jumped backward with an audible cry of fright when Mrs. Chang threw open the door. "You jumpy like old mule tonight, Miss Brittany."

"I—I was daydreaming, Mrs. Chang, and not at all prepared for your efficiency. I hadn't rung the doorbell yet."

"Mr. Kennedy here with new woman. He don't bother you now." The Chinese housekeeper fixed her dark luminous eyes on Brit's face and smiled.

Brit answered the gleam in them with a sprinkle of laughter. "Good. You finally paired him with someone else. Do you approve of his choice this time?"

The old woman nodded. "This one, she the right one. Now we find man for you."

"Here she is, Marion, and you'll have to share the limelight with her. Brittany looks like one of those Paris models tonight." Lewis entered the reception hall in a billow of pipe smoke, one hand extended to welcome her officially.

"Hello, Lewis. Sorry to be late. Am I the last guest to arrive?"

"Not at all. There are no special hours tonight; we have a buffet. How are you, my dear?" He kissed her and propelled her into the hall with one hand behind her waist.

"I'm fine, thank you." She returned the greeting with the old standby reply, and smiled at his wife. Tonight was not the time to go into the failures of her love-life. "Happy Birthday, Miss Marion. You look

172

younger and more radiant than I've ever seen you before. Are you starting a new trend for the older generation to follow?"

"You sweet girl, what a lovely thing to say. If I do seem younger, it's due to you and Mitchell, and to my wonderfully invigorating job. It keeps me on my toes, and I love it." She bobbed up and down a few times to demonstrate.

Brittany joined Lewis in appreciation of her frivolity, and then presented her gift. "This is only part of it. You'll get the rest in installments."

"What can it be?" Marion carried the package to an antique settee, and perched on the edge of it while removing the ribbon and gift wrap. "I'm always tempted to keep such beautiful packages unopened; it seems such a tragedy to dismantle them when the bows and papers are so exquisitely put together. The temptation doesn't last long, of course." She twinkled her eyes at them.

"Marion is worse than a child when it comes to presents. She adores them," Lewis explained, nudging Brittany.

"What did you give her this year, Lewis?"

"He was generous to a fault, dear, and wonderfully clever. He presented me with an itinerary for a fall trip to China. It was tucked inside a lovely piece of luggage, gloriously lightweight and expandable, and with the added marvel of wheels! It's truly remarkable what ingenious products are on the market today."

Marion pulled the cover from the gift box, and removed the tissue paper with a quick eager movement. "What's this? Lewis, come see! Brittany has filled an album with pictures of the Casebolt House. Look. It begins with the street view. Oh, and here are the rooms before we began the restoration and decoration."

Brittany let her leaf through the pages and discover each surprise on her own.

"Look, Lewis. Here's the daughter's bedroom at each stage from beginning to end."

"Not quite the end, Miss Marion," Brit corrected. "We'll take more pictures tomorrow after you've had all the furniture and accessories arranged. Maybe we can even add a picture of Hally when she arrives. We'll do the same for every room in the house, and when you finish in early fall, you'll have an accurate accounting of your hard work. I hope it'll make a happy memory someday."

With tear-filled eyes, Marion expressed her gratitude. "With all you have to do, how did you ever have time to think of this? I'll treasure it always. Thank you, Brittany."

"You're welcome. I'm glad you like it." Brit walked with the Stanfords into the sumptuous living room, and felt a wave of panic when a sea of eyes turned in their direction. A cheer went up as if on cue, and the throng of jubilant guests broke into a rousing rendition of the birthday song.

Brittany hated being in the limelight. *He* might be out there, condemning her with his eyes. Already, the moisture was accumulating in the palms of her hands. She joined the singing with less enthusiasm than she would have under different circumstances, and worked her way down the two steps into the room to lose herself among the singers.

She mustn't let the thought of Mitch being somewhere in the house ruin the entire evening for her. Running and hiding never accomplished a thing. She couldn't become a hermit, fearing to leave the safety of her apartment in case she should chance to meet him. For all she knew, he had declined the invitation tonight. In all likelihood, he had a previous engagement with his betrothed.

The worst thing that could happen would be confronting him in this room full of people. And what could he possibly say or do to upset her in a crowd? There was safety in numbers.

Brittany accepted a glass of punch from the tray of a butler moving past her, and worked her way toward the open doors leading out onto a covered patio. Somewhere on the property, Doug Kennedy was dancing attendance on his intended bride. It was time to meet her.

Strolling the circumference of the patio, she found a secluded place to sit on a low rock wall dividing it from the formal gardens. She gazed contentedly about her, fully relaxed for the first time in weeks. Most of the guests at the party were contemporaries of Marion and Lewis. She recognized many with names which were household words to knowledgeable San Francisco natives. They were active, successful people who used their money and power to preserve and enhance every phase of life imaginable in the Bay city. Several were widows.

Suddenly, a familiar laugh drew Brittany's attention to the living room just inside the french doors. Doug Kennedy was under the rapt spell of a lovely strawberry blond with delicate features and a slender build. He held one of her hands in both of his, and his gleaming, green eyes were glued to her glowing face. Lucky, lucky Georgina Warren. Doug loved her. He would be a nice, decent, wholesome husband, attentive to her needs, appreciative of her talents, and always quick to bring laughter to her lips.

"Looks like your love has found himself a new conquest. I didn't think he was the type to play the field." The sarcasm in the deep-pitched voice speaking into her ear was as startling to Brit as the immediate recognition of who spoke the despicable words.

Bracing her shoulders to fend off the surprise attack, she finished the punch in her glass before turning to cast Mitch Newmann a look of hostility. "Doug is in love with Georgina, and wants to marry her."

175

"Does she know he practices on you in his spare time?"

Brittany's lips parted in astonishment and anger. "That's a cheap shot, Mitchell Newmann, and unworthy of both Doug and me." A bitter resentment crept into her voice. "You've changed into someone I'm almost ashamed to know. You used to treat people fairly. Doug is not a two-timer, and for your information, has never kissed me. No man has, except you. I am still *untried* in every way. You can raise your eyebrows all you want; I have nothing to lose by speaking the truth. I've saved myself all these years, and I might as well hang on a little longer. There's bound to be some decent, Christian man left who will appreciate a virgin bride and treasure her gift of love enough to provide a wedding ring. I'm going to hold out for the whole shooting match, Mr. Newmann—a white gown, a church wedding, family and friends to witness what will be the happiest day of my life, and a real home with an adoring husband, kids, and pets. You might say I'm as Victorian as the houses I like to restore! One thing for sure, I don't intend to give up my belief in God's blueprint for love and marriage for *anyone*, even if I have to be an old maid—as you so nicely called me one other night—the rest of my life!"

Brittany finished her speech on her feet, with her chest heaving and her breath coming in uneven spurts of rage. She wasn't far from tears, and could feel hot color stain her cheeks. Mitch studied her in silence, but the tension between them crackled. Her hand was curled so tightly around the empty punch glass, she was afraid it would break. Marion's birthday party was no place for a repeat performance of the last time Mitch's words had shocked her.

Pushing the glass at him with an angry thrust, she fumed, "Here. Find some place to put it. I'm getting out of this place before I'm tempted to throw it! I'm going to go home and pray that God will give me the grace to forgive you. And then I'm going to pray that He'll knock some sense into you and remove the blinders from your eyes!''

Late the next evening, Brittany placed a bouquet of freshly-cut spring flowers on the tea table near the Victorian loveseat in Mrs. Newmann's bedroom, and stepped back to the door for a final look. The room was lovely enough to grace the pages of *Architectural Digest*, in her humble opinion, but she wouldn't be content without a favorable comment from the woman who would live out her final days there.

Surely a woman who had once chosen such timeless pieces of quality furniture, and then preserved them with the care these showed, would find the new setting for them enchanting. The room suggested one from the Victorian era, but it was without the clutter. Using several paintings from Mrs. Newmann's water-color collection as a guide to her interests and tastes, Marion had chosen a beautiful Aubusson carpet with a multitude of soft shadings in pinks and greens as a starting point. Flowered Victorian chintzes covered the fourposter mahogany bed, the chairs, and a small couch. Needlepoint cushions were scattered about, a few lace doilies graced table tops along with choice pieces of family memorabilia, and now, with the addition of fresh flowers, the room reflected the spirit of a private, indoor garden.

Satisfied that the room was as perfect as she could make it, Brittany snapped off the lamp lights and closed the door. She had already made similar checks of Hally's room and the master suite. Nothing had escaped her attention. It was time to lock up and go back to her apartment. Mitch's family was due to arrive in a few short hours. She would have to wait out the weekend before learning if Mitch wanted her back on Monday to continue with the remainder of the house.

To her surprise, a seething blanket of thick fog wrapped its way around her when she stepped outside the back door, completely obliterating even her shoes from sight. She had stayed too late, and ignored the warnings from the weather bureau broadcast over the car radio that morning.

San Francisco suffered frequently from hazardous fogs, produced whenever warm Pacific winds met cold water along the northern California coast. It happened especially in the summer months. Fog would tumble over the hills, and sift low under the Golden Gate bridge, filling the city and the bay with a gauze curtain of almost impenetrable density. Throughout the history of the area, the mournful overture of foghorns guiding the steady stream of ships through the narrow river channels and into the port had lulled the residents to sleep. They would certainly sing tonight.

Brittany stood on the steps feeling utterly helpless. For several minutes, she stared through the ghostly shroud, too tired to think. Rallying herself took a special effort, and all it accomplished was to send her back into the house. After her eyes adjusted to the sudden burst of light when she flicked on the wall switch, she continued to stare wearily, this time at the pine planks of the kitchen floor.

Her options were limited to only one. She was fogbound. She would have to spend the night in Casebolt House, and leave as soon as there was clear visibility in the morning.

Brit sighed several times—heavy, lengthy sighs. She had put in a long day, but since that wasn't unusual in her line of work, it didn't make sense to feel so exhausted that she couldn't move. The way she felt right now, if there were a cot in front of her, she would fall forward on her nose and sleep right where she was.

She was in Mitch Newmann's house—that was the

real problem. In a few hours his mother and daughter would join him here. The house would take on the personality of its inhabitants, and from now on, each day she came here to oversee the restoration, she would feel Mitch's presence. She would know what he ate for breakfast, what the cook was preparing for his supper, whether or not he was entertaining, or going out for the evening. She would go past his bedroom and see personal items reminding her of the intimate facets of his life. And one day—perhaps very soon—she might have to take orders from his new wife.

Brit covered her trembling lips with the fingers of one equally shaky hand, and squeezed her eyes tightly against the pain of that vision. How well she was able to deal with the trauma would reflect on her entire future. Her love for Mitch had to be put in the proper perspective—and maybe laid to rest permanently. There was so much more to life than mourning over a lost love, and there was no doubt in her mind that life was worth living. Why couldn't she do what her mind knew needed to be done!

Lord, on days like this I feel like I'm battling my way through doubts and a lack of faith as dense as the fog. Satan never gives up, does he? Well, I intend to keep You number one in my life, and although I've been preoccupied with thoughts of Mitch, and spent weeks feeling sorry for myself, I know deep inside that my life will be full and rich even without him. I'm just like Your disciples that day when You were caught in a storm on the Sea of Galilee. They were afraid for their lives and You rebuked them for their lack of faith. Lord, you have promised Your children, 'I am with you always, even unto the end.' and 'I will never leave you, nor forsake you.' I'm going to get through this and live victoriously. I believe You'll take care of me. Thank You for Your love and willing forgiveness. Bring peace to my life, Lord, and to Mitch's too. Take

*the bitterness and hurt from his heart, and forgive him
for forgetting he has everything he needs in life if he
has You.*

Brittany's brief reminder of God's love was enough
to refuel her store of energy, and put her into motion.
After placing her purse and portfolio on a counter, she
headed straight for the refrigerator. Not even much-
needed sleep could take precedence over filling her
empty stomach. Next to being loved and receiving
satisfaction from her work, she liked to eat. Food
made her feel good. Food had a way of making even
the most unsolvable problem diminish in importance
. . . at least for a short time. At the moment, she
needed a feast.

Seated in one of the antique oak rockers in front of
the unlit kitchen fireplace, Brit munched on a giant
sandwich and a fruit salad. She felt like Goldilocks in
the house of the Three Bears. In fact, the picture it
conjured up brought up her next problem—where she
should sleep. Quickly she decided on the couch in the
upstairs sitting room.

A few minutes later, she found some extra blankets
and a pillow in the closet, shut the door, removed her
shoes, and snuggled onto her make-shift bed. While
tears rolled quietly down her cheeks, she thanked God
once again for letting her know Mitch at all, and
pleaded for peace of mind. Before falling into a sound
sleep she reminded herself that she didn't have an
alarm clock. She would have to rely on her inbuilt
sense of timing. It was of paramount importance she
be up and gone before the arrival of Mitchell Newmann and his family.

CHAPTER 11

BRITTANY AWOKE RELUCTANTLY several hours later, but lay without stirring on the couch. Her body felt leaden.

A light ticklish feeling on the sole of one foot roused her, and her eyes fluttered open to find the room drenched with sunlight. She had overslept! The possible repercussion of that error galvenized her into action and she sat bolt upright.

"Good morning."

"Mitch?" Her first spoken word was a hesitant sleep-fogged croak. Was she still asleep? *"Mitch!"* she echoed, rubbing her eyes with hastily-applied knuckles before looking again. He was real! "Wh–what are you doing here?"

"Waking a sleeping beauty."

He moved one hand to trace a featherweight line down the bottom of her foot again. Sometime during the night, she had kicked off the blanket and Mitch was sitting on it at the end of the couch.

"H–how long have you been here?" she stammered weakly, pulling up her knees and wrapping her arms around them. She needed to busy herself with anything to keep from meeting his disconcerting silver-grey gaze.

"Long enough. I've enjoyed just looking at you, stretched out in your pale pink sweater dress, with your gorgeous mass of black hair tumbling over the pillow in disarray, and your face. . . . You're more beautiful than Michelangelo's famous sleeping beauty on the Medici tombs: Night . . . and every bit as mysterious."

The picture Mitch created of her sleeping under his watchful gaze made her conscious of how she must look now with her face shiny and with messed make-up, her eyes drowsy with sleep, and her dark curly hair so thoroughly disheveled.

"I—I had to stay here last night because of the fog," she explained, her hazel eyes huge and clearly distraught.

"That's what we gathered when we opened the door to find you here."

"W—we?"

"Yes, *we*. What's the matter, Brit, aren't you quite awake?" His grey eyes laughed at her confusion. "I was taking my mother and daughter on a grand tour."

"Oh . . ." Brittany buried her scarlet face against her knees. "What did they say? Who did you tell them I was?" she exclaimed, her words muffled against the fabric of her dress.

"I told them you were the architect responsible for the restoration, and had probably been stranded here by the heavy fog. Mother said I had good taste and Hally's exact words were, "Wow, she's gorgeous." They're downstairs getting acquainted with the household staff you hired, and organizing a celebration brunch for us. It's almost eleven o'clock. I'm afraid you had quite a long sleep. I told them to give us a few minutes alone because we had some unfinished business to settle."

Brittany shifted positions but not for the life of her could she lift her head to look at him. What did he mean by celebration brunch? Was it really almost noon? What business . . . ?

"Are you listening to me, Gypsy?"

"Yes."

"Mother and Hally are eager to meet you, Gypsy, because I also told them . . ." He stopped to move nearer, and she could feel her heart pounding. "I told them that you . . ." he repeated, his faintly husky voice close to her ear.

He knew what he was doing to her. He was close enough to see the trembling of her limbs, to hear the wild pulse-beats of her drumming heart, to feel the stoppage of her breathing while she waited for him to finish. The silence stretched, and with her face still buried against her knees, she waited—waited for him to continue.

"I told Mother and Hally you were the woman I loved more than my life, and second only to God," he finished, his breath stirring her hair and caressing her ear.

It seemed an eternity before his words registered through the swamping tidal wave of emotions she was experiencing. Fighting against the need to cry, she raised her head far enough to peek through the heavy veil of her long hair. "Wh—what did you say, Mitch?" she whispered, her voice choking on a swallowed sob.

His hands reached up to smooth back her hair, freeing her entire face to his view, and his smokey eyes roamed possessively over every feature. His trembling fingers traced the shape of her brows, the length of her long cheekbones, the gentle slope of her almost-perfect nose, and the faint hollows that deepened whenever laughter creased them. His voice was husky when he repeated his ardent declaration. "I said, I love you with all my heart, Gypsy."

183

Left with only a remnant of her sanity, she was, for a moment, almost too terrified to touch him. What if this was only a cruel joke? What if he intended to elicit a similar admission from her, and then cast her aside? What if . . . "You're s—sure? You're not just saying it to . . ."

He silenced her question with a finger against her quivering lips. "I've only half lived since you left me in Baltimore, my darling. I tried to find you for several months, but every lead came to a dead end. At first, I buried myself in my work, but at the end of every long day, I still had to return to an empty apartment, and the loneliness was excruciating." His shadowed eyes examined her face a few seconds longer, before he finally turned away.

"I stopped praying for your return, and blamed God for punishing me more severely than I deserved. I had already lost a wife and suffered the loneliness of the heart, I couldn't understand why I should have to lose you, too. Well-meaning friends introduced me to others, but none could measure up to my memories of you. Finally, I gave up dating altogether. I lost interest in my work, and daughter . . . everything."

He loved her! All the past pain and grief and suffering fell from Brit. She wanted to run and leap and shout, and proclaim to the world that her heart had wings. She wanted to ring bells over the city, and stand at the top of Nob Hill and . . .

"I love you, Mitch! I love you, I love you, I love you!" Tears of joy rolled from under her lashes.

Mitch embraced her tightly. "Be mine forever," he murmured, his voice husky and unsteady. "I love you, Brit." He smiled, and brushed a strand of hair from her cheek.

Brittany could feel the stirring within herself. She wanted his strong arms around her body to stop the trembling. Was she finally going to hear a proposal?

"Do you think one week is long enough to arrange a

184

wedding?'' He captured her trembling lips in a long probing kiss before continuing. "I'd give you the stars and the moon on a silver platter, if it were possible; but will you settle for a simple church wedding? We'll call your folks, dear, and have them gather everyone together to fly out here in a chartered plane.''

Brit willed herself not to cry, but the tenderness in Mitch's voice, the blazing light in his eyes, the wonder of his incredible words were too powerful.

Mitch smiled. "I want to give you the whole shooting match, my wild, dark-eyed gypsy—including this home, Hally, and as many brothers and sisters as you're willing to provide for her. And most of all, an adoring husband who promises to love his Victorian-principled, sweet, tender-hearted, hard-working, lovely, God-fearing wife without ceasing until the day he dies. Did I forget anything?''

She tried to tell him 'no' in words, but had to stop and shake her head instead. He had remembered every word of her impassioned speech at Marion's birthday party.

He held her hands tightly between his, and sought her eyes again. "It's my prayer now, darling, that you can forgive me for taking so long to come to my senses.'' His voice was solemn, and hesitant. "After your well-deserved chastisement the other night, I went back to my hotel room for some hard soul-searching. I had a lengthy list of sins to confess, but thankfully, our Heavenly Father stands ready to forgive. When Lewis first brought you to Casebolt House, I couldn't believe my good fortune. I had resigned myself to living without you.''

He cleared his throat, swallowing audibly. "When you rejected me a second time, with the stunning declaration that you couldn't be involved with a *family* man, I resolved to stay away from you. I knew I couldn't marry anyone who wouldn't accept my daughter as her own . . . even though I had been a poor father to her.''

"Oh, Mitch, it was all such a tragic mistake," Brit injected impassionately. "I should have trusted you as much as I loved you. I should have waited for an explanation, but when I saw those pictures in your bedroom, I thought you were a married man with a child, and . . ."

". . .and cheating on them both while away from home. I can't blame you for thinking that," Mitch finished for her. "It seems to be a common practice these days. It was my fault entirely, darling. I should have told you about them, but I had grieved for three years, and thought I could never love again. And then you came into my life like a breath of sunshine. I selfishly chose to enjoy only the present, and dream of the future with you. I've always been a man of few words. As you can tell, I'm trying to reform."

"I was hurt and angry, and beside myself with anguish, Mitch," Brit said, softly caressing his face. "I thought you had betrayed me; but even then, I needed the entire width of the country to keep myself from returning to you. It was the greatest testing of my Christian faith to stay away. I couldn't willfully break God's commandments. Then, when I discovered you had been a *widower* all those years, I was . . ."

"Did you honestly not know until that night at the Stanford's?"

She shook her head, tears swimming around her eyes once again. "I was stunned to hear you say that. All I knew was that I still loved you, and I prayed constantly that God would help me win back your love and trust. It just had to be His will that we share our lives."

For a moment, they had to stop and reconfirm that their love had survived intact, and even grown, throughout the tragic separation.

"Mitch," Brit murmured, after re-emerging from under the spell of his gaze, "I thought you were engaged to marry Alexis."

He chuckled. "I noticed she was eager to give you that impression, and shamelessly used her interest in me as a shield against you. I fully intended to make you suffer for turning me down. In spite of all my well-argued intentions, I was helpless against my love for you."

"But, you even met with Reverend. Katkov."

"Alexis is president of the Bay Association, and Katkov is chairman of the division in charge of the area where my re-development project is to be located. My meetings with them were purely business and goodwill sessions. How about Doug Kennedy? I was insanely jealous of that guy's relationship with you. I hired him originally to keep him away from you, and even went so far as to hire Georgina as a hopeful diversion. It must have been the workings of the Lord that made everything turn out so well."

Pleased with knowledge of the extent of Mitch's love, Brit laughed gleefully. "Doug is like a brother to me," she explained after sobering, "protective and supportive; but he's madly in love with Georgina. Mitch . . ." she trailed her fingers down the tanned column of his neck and paused to gently tug on the collar of his shirt. "Mitch, what made you finally decide you wanted to marry me?"

"You want to hear it all, do you?" He stopped the movement of her hand and brought it to his lips, kissing each finger with a caress. "I built up a month-long accumulation of reasons why I shouldn't pursue my love for you. There was Doug. He's younger and childless. There was your career. You have enormous talent, and are destined for widespread renown. There was Hally. You obviously enjoyed working, and I thought mothering Hally and children of your own would be far down on your list of priorities."

While he spoke, Brit suffered each moment of suffering and doubts he had experienced. "One by one, you battered down my arguments, and reminded me why I had chosen to love you in the first place. You shared my interest in preserving the architecture of the past, while recognizing the importance of reclaiming blighted areas for coming generations. You reminded me of my parental responsibilities to Hally with bewildering defensiveness of her needs, and then reinforced your beliefs with the miraculous rebirthing of Casebolt House into a beautiful home that reflected your true feelings for her. She showed me the enormous stuffed poodle you bought for her bed, and the personal note you attached to its collar promising her a real puppy if I granted permission. How could I not love you for that?"

"I thought the puppy would provide companionship until she has an opportunity to make new friends in the fall."

"See what I mean? You'll make a wonderful new mother. I saw the flowers and the note you gave to my mother, too. The tears came to her eyes when she saw her room. Everywhere I looked, there was another indication of your thoughtfulness and understanding of her importance to me and to Hally."

"I love you, Mitch. You daughter and your mother are a part of you, and I wanted you to know I cared."

"The message finally got through to me. I realized you have the amazing ability to juggle a career, *and* fill a home with all the love and attention its members need. I probably wouldn't have been able to see this without that marvelous little speech of yours, though. God used you to speak to my heart. When you declared your intention to have a *family* life . . ."

His mouth found hers again, and their deep feelings for each other were made known.

"Daddy?" A hesitant knocking accompanied the noticeably embarrassed inquiry outside the sitting room door. "Grandma asked me to remind you we'll be ready to eat soon."

Mitch smiled at Brit, and raked his shaking fingers

through tousled dark hair. "Tell her we'll be down in a few minutes," he instructed Hally.

"Will she like me, Mitch?" Hearing the deadline for their first meeting started a whole new series of uneasy flutterings in the pit of Brittany's stomach.

"She'll adore you, especially if you ask her to be a bridesmaid in our wedding. One of the greatest thrills I'll ever have as her father is to present her with a new mother who shares the same Christian faith and ideals of her mother and grandmother. If Hally can combine what she's learned from them with any one of your endearing traits, I'll consider myself the luckiest and most blessed man this side of heaven."

"Your mother will approve of me?"

"She already does, but if we aren't downstairs pretty soon, she might change her mind."

"Tell me again that this isn't all a dream, Mitch."

He laughed, and dropped down to the carpet on one knee before her. "My beautiful dark-eyed gypsy, I love you to distraction. Please do me the honor of becoming my wife, the mother of all my children, and the new daughter of my dear mother, who already knows about my great love for you. In return, I promise to cherish you, honor you, take care of you, trust you, bless you, and thank God for you, every single day, the rest of my life."

Brit's heart was filled with an unbearable rapture. She would belong to Mitch. She would be his help-mate as ordained by God. Already, he had her blood singing an aria, and one week from this precious moment, they would sing the ultimate song of love together. They would be fully united, body and soul, forever.

Gathering his head into her arms, she whispered "Do you hear my heart speaking to you, Mitch Newmann? It's shouting my answer in double deci-bels. Yes-yes-yes-yes-yes! I can't believe this is happening. Yesterday, my world was as gloomy and grey as the undulating fog, and now it's colored with the bright and glorious colors of a prism. Yesterday, San Francisco was just a city, and now it's *our* city. Oh, Mitch, from now on, I can love even the days of fog, and welcome their presence in my life without complaint . . . because a night of fog returned the other half of my life to me." Brittany leaned back. "I'm so happy I could die!" she cried in jubilation.

"You don't have time," Mitch laughed, pulling her to her feet. "We have a lunch date in exactly five and a half minutes."

"I'll meet you downstairs in ten," she countered, with the radiance of stars in her eyes. "I need a few minutes alone to thank a very dear Partner and Friend, who kept His word, and answered my prayers."

Mitch smiled with a new tenderness in his eyes, and extended a hand to her. "Let's thank Him together, darling."

ABOUT THE AUTHOR

When NANCY O. JOHANSON isn't traveling around the world with her research physician husband, collecting material for her books, she is busily engaged in writing them. BY LOVE RESTORED is a melding of her interest in homes of the Victorian era and her belief that God is able to heal and restore relationships.

"I have asked God to help me with my writing," Nancy said recently. "If I succeed in nothing else through the publication of this book, I want my children to know it is possible to find that one-worth-waiting-for love if they are patient and abide by their beliefs."

Forever Romances are inspirational romances designed to bring you a joyful, heart-lifting reading experience. If you would like more information about joining our Forever Romance book series, please write to us:

Guideposts Customer Service
39 Seminary Hill Road
Carmel, NY 10512

Forever Romances are chosen by the same staff that prepares *Guideposts,* a monthly magazine filled with true stories of people's adventures in faith. *Guideposts* is not sold on the newsstand. It's available by subscription only. And subscribing is easy. Write to the address above and you can begin reading *Guideposts* soon. When you subscribe, each month you can count on receiving exciting new evidence of God's Presence, His Guidance and His limitless love for all of us.